With Love
And Kisses

Patsy Collins

To Les and Ethel –
the parents of the man I love.

Contents

1. Ad Lib

Jemima ran her manicured hand through her fine, blonde hair and asked, "Will you marry me?"

Andrew almost dropped his script. He blinked and wondered if he'd heard her correctly.

She moved along the sofa so she was sitting with her thigh touching his, took his hand in hers, looked into his eyes and whispered the words again.

Andrew sighed and sat back on the sofa. Everything was almost perfect. They were spending the evening together at her place; which was good. Scented candles provided romantic lighting, the gentle sounds from the stereo added to the atmosphere. That was very good. He was sipping his favourite wine and holding Jemima's hand. Excellent.

Jemima herself was, of course, absolutely perfect. She always was. The words she'd just spoken would have been perfect too, had they been sincere. It wasn't fair; for years she'd been saying things like that to him but never meant a word. She always acted and sounded as though she did, but then Jemima was an excellent actress.

It had started in school. Their drama club had put on a production of Top Gun. Jemima, acting her part, had taken his hand and demanded, "Take me to bed, or lose me forever." He hadn't taken her to bed, of course, but he hadn't lost her either. They'd attended the same drama school and they'd kissed as Romeo and Juliet, frolicked as Antony and Cleopatra, and argued as Fred and Wilma.

As Andrew and Jemima they'd gone out for meals together, helped each other prepare for challenging roles and spent cosy evenings in, drinking wine on her sofa. They had kissed many times, but unless it was on stage or in rehearsal, the kisses where never more than a friendly peck in greeting.

He'd proposed to her on occasion, but only when a role demanded it. Never, under any circumstances, had she proposed to him. Until three minutes ago. He wasn't entirely sure why she'd done it now. There must, he supposed, have been a last minute script change.

"Sorry, just give me a moment," he stalled.

As Andrew scanned the papers in his hands, looking for the words she'd just said, he wished she hadn't insisted they do the read-through by candlelight. It did add to the atmosphere, but it made the actual reading more difficult.

Having her say those words to him made thinking even more difficult. He didn't remember there being a proposal in this play, or any mention of one by the director. He could clearly remember all those he'd made previously and each of her convincing acceptances. Andrew and Jemima were often cast opposite each other. Directors saw they were the perfect couple; why couldn't she?

"Sorry, Jemima. Could you repeat that line?"

"Will you marry me?"

He had heard her right then, this time it wasn't his mind playing tricks like it had in the past. Several times he'd been almost sure she'd whispered, "I love you," during a clinch. It'd just been wishful thinking though; the words weren't scripted. Come to think of it, neither were the words she'd just spoken. If they weren't in his copy, the couldn't be in hers.

"I don't know what's going on," he admitted.

"It seems perfectly clear to me."

"What you said isn't in my copy," he explained waving the script.

"It's not in mine either," she said, putting hers down and taking his other hand. "I asked you if you'll marry me."

"You can't ad lib like that," he said.

"I can't?"

"No, plays have to be carefully scripted."

"OK. But what about life, is it OK to improvise then?"

"Yes, I suppose so, sometimes. It's probably still best to plan things through though."

He was confused. She'd asked him to come round this evening. He'd arrived to find her dressed for the part, and gentle music and soft lighting supplying the atmosphere, but she'd seemed reluctant to rehearse. What was going on?

"Set the scene you mean?" she asked.

"Yes, that kind of thing," he agreed.

"What if the other person won't play their part?"

He wasn't sure if she was still talking about acting. It was probably safest to assume she was.

"Give them a prompt?"

"Good idea," Jemima said and stood up.

She returned with a pen, took Andrew's script from him and crossed out a line of her dialogue. Above it she wrote, 'will you marry me?' Then she crossed out his printed response and replaced it with, 'Yes'. Finally she wrote, 'and they both lived happily ever after' and handed it back to him. "Shall we take it from the top?"

"OK."

"Will you marry me?" she said.

"Yes," he said. "Now take me to bed or lose me forever."

"That's not your line!"

"I'm ad libbing. How do you fancy an undressed rehearsal of the honeymoon?"

2. Fairground Attraction

"Go on, I dare you!" a boy's voice called.

Isabelle turned to see who was daring who to do what. The group of boys were much younger than her, about twelve or fourteen she guessed, enjoying the freedom of a long summer evening at the start of the school holidays. The dare was simply to go on the ghost train and the boy, who was being urged to take a last ride before the fair closed for the night, didn't look scared.

"I will if you will," he threw back at the other boys.

"Come on then, we'll protect you from the scary stuff," the biggest one said. He hunched his back, lifted his arms with fingers spread wide and pushed his jaw to one side in an unconvincing monster impression.

The boys all laughed, the one who was challenged included, and together joined the short queue for the ride. Isabelle smiled as she watched them nudge and jostle each other, wondering if the ghost train would make them jump in mild alarm and be glad to have their friends with them, or if they'd giggle through the whole thing.

Some dares were like that; friends egging each other on to try something new. Often it was just harmless fun, soon forgotten. Isabelle and her friends had probably issued and accepted dozens like that. Occasionally, the dares were less frivolous and had consequences that could last a lifetime. As Isabelle remembered the dare she'd been challenged with, she watched the boys pay their money and scramble into the carriages. The young lads were still laughing; the older girls who'd surrounded Isabelle hadn't laughed. Had they guessed then, even as they said the words, the great impact the challenge would have?

Isabelle walked away from the ghost train toward the dodgems on the far side of the fairground. As she passed the waltzer she couldn't help snapping her fingers and shuffling her feet in time to the rock 'n' roll tune blaring out.

The smaller attractions were already silent and dark. Anyone who'd not yet won a goldfish, enormous glass vase or cuddly life-sized pig had lost their chance until next year. The family groups, the couples, the gangs of friends, streamed past Isabelle as they reluctantly made their way to the exits. The giggles and chatter seemed louder now, as the machinery and music were switched off and the ride operators stopped calling, 'roll up, roll up for the thrill of your life'. She shivered; seeking thrills no longer held the attraction it had when she'd first walked onto the fairground.

A few of the passing crowd were clutching huge prizes they'd won and looking as if they already wished they'd made choices which would be easier to live with. She could understand that, but hoped some of the outsize toys would be kept as mementoes of a happy evening. Good memories shouldn't be lost.

The smell of hotdogs, frying onions and freshly cooked doughnuts wafted about on the warm air. Every corner held a stall offering burgers or chips, ice cream, candyfloss and toffee to sustain the crowds on their journey to the car park. Isabelle wasn't hungry. She hurried on past the Merry-go-Round. The painted horses that, not long ago, circled and pranced were now still and ghostly quiet.

Soon the only people left were the staff. Most were

securing their rides and stalls; covering them with tarpaulins against the weather or pushing home bolts and turning keys as protection from thieves and vandals.

There were now more lights on in the caravans and trailers, that were the homes of the staff, than on the fairground rides. The workers' day was ending and they were preparing for bed. Isabelle walked quietly past, not wanting to wake those already asleep. For a moment, a beam from the security light on the Ferris wheel created a shadow like a giant web around her. She shook the thought away and walked on, increasing her pace just to keep warm.

As Isabelle approached the dodgems her heart raced as fast as it had the first time she'd slid down the Helter Skelter and landed at the feet of an attractive young man in overalls.

"Well done for missing me," he'd said as her mat just brushed his foot.

Isabelle's heart had missed a beat.

"You'd be a natural for the Dodgems," he assured her. "That's where I work."

Of course Isabelle had persuaded her friends to take a ride on the small electric cars. The man's hand touched hers, each time he'd taken her money, sending a charge through her just as the car's masts sent power to their wheels. He'd flirted with Isabelle and bought her candy floss in his break. He'd walked with her, holding her hand and telling her about his life. He'd pointed out the caravan he called home. He'd said he'd like to see her again.

"Go back and see him," her friends had said as they shot air gun pellets at metal ducks. "Go on, we dare you. Wait till the fair is closing up and go and kiss him."

The suggestion had seemed innocent enough when it had

been said in the bright lights and cheerful atmosphere of the noisy fair. Later, in the dark and the quiet, it seemed a lot more daring. She took the last few steps.

"Isabelle, is that you?"

She looked at the man in his oily overalls and said, "Of course it's me and I've come to kiss you."

He stepped down from the closed ride and held his arms out in welcome.

Isabelle kissed him, just as she'd first done as a dare sixty-three years ago, and for every night of their sixty year marriage.

3. Before And After

Louise never looks her best in the mornings and this morning is no exception. Drinking a lot last night won't have helped. Neither will have not getting to sleep until gone three. She hadn't even removed her make-up; she'd had something else on her mind. His name is Lee and he's snoring beside her. Louise doesn't mind the snoring, she thinks it's manly and Louise likes her men to be all man. This one definitely is. He has extremely short hair, broad shoulders, stubbly chin and a tattoo. It's taken a while to get him into her bed but she wasn't disappointed. She hopes he wasn't either.

Aware that streaked mascara and nasty breath aren't appealing, Louise eases the quilt away and moves quietly to the bathroom. Louise guesses Lee is the sort of bloke who likes his girls feminine. Well, she'll do what she can. The bare materials aren't bad; flat stomach, slim hips, breasts almost too perfect to be natural. Her hair is stylishly cut, her nails polished and legs waxed. Louise aims to be all woman. There are some things in life you can't change and some things you can. Louise has made all the changes she reasonably can to ensure she's attractive to men. The things she can't change she tries not to worry about.

Louise isn't exactly a beautiful woman. Her chin is a little on the strong side for one thing, but what she lacks in looks is more than made up for in personality. She has a larger than life quality. Everything about her seems exaggerated.

She often wears a little too much make-up, is usually slightly overdressed. She's the life and soul of every gathering, always ready to tell a joke. People like Louise. She's fun, confident and always up for any mad scheme her friends suggest.

As she cleans and tidies herself she thinks back to the first time she saw Lee. They'd been teenagers waiting for a bus. A slightly older girl had swaggered confidently by, her smooth stocking-encased legs displayed below a very short, emerald green skirt and ending in the highest, pointiest shoes imaginable. The girl's flamboyant blonde hair owed absolutely nothing to nature. She wore so much make-up it was impossible to guess the original skin tone. If her breasts had been pushed up any higher her neck would have been entirely hidden.

"Now that's what I call a real woman!" Lee had declared enthusiastically into the smog of the girl's perfume and cigarette smoke.

Louise had looked down at her own hairy legs, shapeless clothes and scruffy trainers. It was clear there was no comparison.

Lee had changed and matured a lot since. So had Louise. She'd seen him again in a nightclub and approached, intending to thank him for acting as a catalyst for her now happy life. He hadn't recognised her of course, and had offered her a drink as soon as she was near enough for them to speak to each other. Louise decided to thank him not just with words. Gradually the relationship developed and last night, for the first time, they made love.

Once her teeth and face are clean, Louise brushes her hair, then squirts on some perfume. She applies lipstick but decides that's overdoing it so removes it and gets back into bed.

Lee wakes and pulls her into his arms,"Hmm you smell nice." He kisses her. "Taste nice too. If you've brushed your teeth that's cheating."

"So, I cheated, what are you going to do about it?"

His response is to make love to her again. She takes her punishment like a woman.

Louise goes downstairs to make coffee. She takes croissants from the freezer and warms them in the microwave. She pours fresh orange juice into glasses that almost match and spoons apricot jam and butter into little dishes. Once everything is crammed onto a tray, Louise carries it up to her waiting lover. She elbows open the door, managing to set the tray down without dropping anything.

Lee is holding a small pine picture frame containing a photograph of a middle aged couple and a young man on a beach.

"Sorry, found this in the drawer," he gestures to the bedside table. "I was looking for a tissue."

"You don't take sugar do you?"

"No thanks. Is he your brother?"

"No. You can borrow my toothbrush if you want."

"Thanks, I'll have a shower after breakfast if that's OK?"

Louise nods her agreement and they eat the croissants. Lee drips jam onto Louise and playfully licks it off. When they've finished breakfast, Lee reluctantly drags himself into the bathroom for a shower. Whilst he washes, Louise removes the crumbs and dirty crockery. She returns to bed, and turns down the quilt, in what she hopes is an inviting manner.

Lee stands looking down at Louise. The small towel

wrapped round his waist does little to conceal his gorgeous body.

"Not your brother then, the chap in the photo?"

"No."

"Your parents though?"

"Yes."

"So who is he, a husband you haven't told me about?" He laughs but doesn't look amused.

"No, but there is something I haven't told you."

"Come on then, Louise, out with it. Who is he?"

"It's not so much who he is, as who he was."

"Oh no! He's dead, you loved him and he died."

"No, Lee, nothing as shocking as that. His name was Lewis, that picture was taken years ago."

"What happened to him?"

"You did."

Lee frowned. "Explain."

"I saw you years ago, waiting for a bus. You admired a pretty girl. I wanted that admiration. It took a lot of time and effort but I've got it now, haven't I?"

"Well, yes. But that doesn't explain the picture."

"It's me. The day after it was taken was the day I knew I finally made my decision to undergo the sex change process."

4. You Can Always Get Another

Jacqui knew something was wrong as soon as she opened the front door. Her beloved cat Minty wasn't there to welcome her. That hadn't been uncommon when Minty was younger, but for the last year or so she'd rarely gone further than the garden and was always inside when Jacqui returned from work.

She found the cat curled up in her basket. Minty purred when Jacqui stroked her soft grey fur but didn't take any notice of the offered food.

Jacqui phoned her boyfriend. "Sorry, Gerry but I'm going to have to cancel our date tonight."

"What's happened?"

"It's Minty. She's not well again."

"You can't help and I've already paid for the tickets."

He was right in a way. Minty went off her food a few weeks ago. The vet said it was just age and she didn't have long left. All Jacqui could do was ensure she didn't suffer at the end. Minty had rallied, but Jacqui had known it was a temporary reprieve.

"I don't want to leave her."

He sighed. "I'll see if my brother wants to come instead."

"Do that. And don't worry about us."

"Oh ... I'm sure it will be fine. I'll call you later, OK?"

Jacqui made herself a cup of tea, fetched a cushion and

sat on the kitchen floor next to Minty. The cat continued to purr softly until she died about an hour later. Tears dripped down Jacqui's face as she told herself it was for the best. Minty had enjoyed a long, healthy life with Jacqui since they were kitten and schoolgirl. She was glad Minty didn't suffer, but knew she'd miss her terribly.

She was still sitting on the kitchen floor when Gerry called her back.

"She's gone. Minty slipped away peacefully."

"Great, we can go away for weekends and stuff now you're not tied to it."

"Great?"

"Sorry, didn't mean to be tactless, but it's not exactly a shock is it? You said it was really old, that's why you couldn't leave it for long."

"Yes, she was old but that doesn't mean I'm not upset."

"Right. Sorry." When she didn't reply he added, "I'll buy you another one if you like."

"Cats aren't like phones, to be replaced with a new model if they get lost."

"No. So what about going out tonight? There'd still be time ..."

"No! Look, I'll call you at the weekend." She disconnected and phoned her parents.

Jacqui felt better after chatting with them. Afterwards she made herself a sandwich and tried to read. Her mind kept drifting to thoughts of Minty and Gerry. He was right that losing her wasn't such a shock. He wasn't quite right about Jacqui not going away with him because of Minty though. Her mum would have been happy to look after her. No, she'd used that as an excuse to avoid jumping when he said, of not always falling in with his plans. Minty had unknowingly protected her from being swept along with everything Gerry wanted.

At work the next day Jacqui's colleagues saw she was upset and were kind when she told them why, especially Carl. Everyone was horrified about the heartless way Gerry had behaved, especially Carl.

As she prepared to leave that afternoon, Carl stopped her to ask if he could do anything to help.

"Thanks, but I'm going to take her to my parents' house and bury her. Her mother is buried there so it seems fitting."

"That's a good plan. You don't drive though, do you? I could take you."

"It's fifty miles, Carl."

"That's no problem."

It was for her. She knew Carl liked her, but she already had a boyfriend so shouldn't encourage him, nor take advantage of his kindness.

"Dad's going to come and get me this evening."

"Good. Still, I can't let you go home alone to face …"

He didn't need to finish the sentence. It had been awful walking into the kitchen that morning and seeing Minty dead in her basket. Jacqui was dreading going home to the same thing.

"Let me drive you home and stay with you until your dad arrives."

Jacqui's hand shook as she tried to unlock her front door. Carl squeezed her shoulder. It helped, even so she cried when she went into the kitchen. Carl held her until her sobs subsided, then made them both a cup of tea.

After they'd drunk it Jacqui fetched a cardboard box Minty had sometimes slept in on her desk while she used her computer. She lined it with a soft towel and took it into the kitchen. Jacqui stroked Minty's head but couldn't bring herself to lift the lifeless body.

Carl gently placed Minty in the box.

"Thank you. I'd better pack up her stuff. I won't want to see her basket when I come home without her."

"No of course not. There's a rescue place near me, I can take everything there if you like?"

"Thanks, that's kind."

"Do you have cat food in the cupboards? You won't want to come across that." Carl took everything out to his car, then sat with her until her parents came.

They buried Minty next to her mother under the apple tree. Afterwards her parents got out photo albums and they looked at pictures of Minty as a kitten and others of the cat with Jacqui as she grew up.

"Things will be so different without her around," Mum said.

"You're right about things being different and not just because of Minty. I've decided to finish with Gerry."

"Good."

"Good?"

"Yes, I'm sorry to be tactless … what?" She broke off as Jacqui laughed.

"Sorry, Mum it's just that's pretty much what Gerry said when I told him about Minty."

"Oh! Well, that proves I'm right."

"So will we be seeing more of that Carl chap?" Dad asked.

"Leave her be. Obviously Gerry hurt her, she's not going to want to risk that again so soon."

"Actually, I might. Carl's nothing like Gerry." Jacqui said. After all boyfriends aren't like cats; if things didn't work out with one, he could easily be replaced.

5. A Real Winner

Julia Colgan had always been a loser. It started thirty-seven seconds before her birth; Julia had the newspaper cuttings to prove it. 'Local girl loses out,' it said. Her mum had been expected to deliver the first baby at the newly opened maternity hospital. Local businesses had promised all kinds of birthday gifts for the first child; photographs by the portrait photographer, clothes, shoes and nappies from children's shops; bottles, sterilising fluid and rusks. If it was needed or wanted for a baby and there was a business in town which supplied it, the first new arrival would receive it.

A woman travelling through the town to visit relations had gone in to premature labour. Mrs Colgan gave birth to Julia, less than a minute after that winning first baby.

Julia was teased at school by the more popular kids. When she couldn't jump over the elastic stretched around the other girl's shoulders, or blinked first in the staring competitions they chanted, "Julia's the loser, Julia's the loser." Pretty, clever, sporty Mary Walters always lead those taunts.

Julia was fascinated by bizarre facts and trivia. Instead of passing silly notes or carving her name in the desk, she'd be writing down snippets of information and trying to remember obscure facts. It wasn't just because of her lack of skill in the games that they teased her; it was because she was openly interested in what the teachers had to say. She wasn't particularly clever, no good at tests or exams; so she was despised by the clever kids too.

"Oh dear, doesn't the *Guinness Book of Records* cover fractions?" Mary sneered.

Julia couldn't calculate percentages or conjugate a verb. She could remember things that interested her. The seven times table bored her and was forgotten but she remembered the names of the seven wonders of the world and where they could be found. She couldn't spell receipt and necessary, but had no trouble with the longest word she could find in dictionary: antidisestablishmentarianism.

After leaving school, she was determined to prove she wasn't the loser everyone said she was, so learnt to put her knowledge to good use. She impressed her family with her ability to answer the odd question on university challenge, or get right the 'Who Wants to be a Millionaire?' question that stumped the contestant.

"How d'you know that, Julia lovey?" her mum would ask.

"You're loads better than that lot, it's you who should be on the telly," her dad said as he patted her hand.

Encouraged by their praise she began to enter competitions in magazines, newspapers and on the internet. Her first prize was a three course meal for two. She won it in a competition run by the local paper. A junior reporter was sent to interview her: Mary Walters.

"Congratulations, Julia," she said without enthusiasm. "You were lucky."

Julia knew it was more than luck; when the editor had phoned, he'd said she'd been the only entrant to answer every question correctly.

From then on, Julia spent all her free time entering

competitions. If the prize was no use to her, she gave it away. The year's supply of cat food was given to her neighbour. Her parent's were thrilled with a weekend's hotel accommodation. Soon it seemed everyone was interested in Julia's competitions.

"Interesting hat, Julia. Did you win it?" neighbours asked when she displayed her latest prize.

"Won anything exciting lately, Julia?" asked John, a man she knew at work.

Julia had and told him about her recent successes.

"Lucky you, you never know when a spare flask or a windup torch will come in handy."

Remembering he was a keen bird-watcher she gave those prizes to him.

She'd never have to buy a light bulb ever again, as she'd won four dozen long-life, energy saving ones. She'd won pink socks, ice skating lessons, four dictionaries. Any day the post could bring news of yet another amazing win.

Julia didn't just win prizes. Her enthusiasm and generosity won her many friends. They in turn brought her details of new competitions or provided answers. John, the bird-watcher, could answer anything about wildlife and natural history. He was flattered when she sought him out to ask.

"We make a good pair, don't we?" he said.

Julia wasn't sure if he just meant their ability to answer questions, until he offered to take her bird-watching with him.

"It'd be great to have some interesting company. We could answer questions whilst we wait for the Reed Warblers to appear and then maybe go for a meal afterwards, that's if you'd like."

His voice faded as he'd spoken, so Julia had to lean close to catch his words.

"Yes please," she'd whispered in reply.

When she won a trip for two to the Caribbean, John went too. He came home with photos of tropical birds. She came home with a bottle of rum she'd won in the hotel's quiz – and an engagement ring!

The editor of the local paper heard about her continued success and asked if he could send Mary Walters to interview her. As he also offered to put her into a special prize draw, for all contributors and featured readers and send a free copy of the paper, Julia agreed.

She opened the copy she'd been presented with and looked again at the double-page spread. The picture of her was quite flattering, especially as the mound of prizes hid her rather wide hips. It wasn't the picture that made her happiest though, it wasn't the report either, despite it giving details of her cleverness. No; what she liked best was the headline Mary had used: 'Julia Colgan is a real winner'.

6. Uncle Mick

Lucy couldn't believe it had come to this, looking for a man in the frozen food section of her local supermarket. She decided that even if the men she'd seen had actually all been available to take home, she would still have left alone. The best specimen was looking at her as if he didn't exactly consider her to be bargain of the week either. Lucy couldn't blame him she decided, as she began piling her purchases onto the belt for the check-out person to scan. Her local supermarket had a singles evening the first Tuesday of each month. It was a marketing gimmick for the sad and lonely. That, Lucy told herself, was not why she was there. She needed to buy groceries. This shop was on her way home and at least on singles nights the queues moved quickly.

Of course the supermarket didn't turn away any potential customers just because they were part of a couple, but anyone not looking for love tended to avoid shopping that night so as not to attract unwelcome attention. Most of the customers at these things were either spotty students or no longer young. The women wore too much make-up and not enough skirt. The men had ponytails; it wasn't nice. Those who were trying hard, filled their baskets with smoked salmon, organic strawberries and chablis. Lucy placed her tampons next to her anti-dandruff shampoo, and then added a couple of tins of own label beans. Her heart wasn't really in this at all and she'd have stayed at home had she not promised her friend Sally that she'd go out somewhere there was at least a chance she could meet someone.

The only offer she got was, "D'you want help packing?"

As the thin youth who made the enquiry then proceeded to wipe the back of his hand under his dripping nose she rejected even this grudging proposition. When she had to report to her friend Sally on 'progress towards getting a man' she wasn't entirely sure this was going to count. Sally herself was completely loved up and thought it was her duty to ensure as many of her friends as possible were in similar bliss.

Lucy's problem, she mused, was that she was a romantic. She expected (or at least hoped) that love would come and sweep her off her feet. She wasn't completely unrealistic; she knew no one was perfect and that relationships take work. She just wanted that initial spark of mutual attraction. She wanted to be in love with a nice man who loved her.

"Is that too much to ask?" she enquired of Sally at work the following day.

"Course not, everyone should be in love, just like me and Malc. Do you want to see the poem he wrote me?"

Lucy hastily offered Sally the last sugary doughnut. She was sure Malcolm had many admirable qualities, but having heard a sample before she knew poetry wasn't his strong point, (or if it was, Sally was in trouble). Sally held a serviette under her chin to catch any jam that might escape from her doughnut and tried to make sympathetic sounds. Their morning break was over and they left the canteen.

"Look, sorry the supermarket thing didn't work, but it was always a bit of a long shot. I've done all I can for you without success, now it's time for drastic action."

"What do you mean by drastic?"

"Don't panic, I just meant we have to get Uncle Mick on

the case."

They were not able to continue the conversation as at least one of them and usually both were busy all morning.

"Portsmouth City Council, how may I help you?" She might just as well have said directory enquiries or Samaritans, they got such a varied range of queries.

"My great granddad was killed in the Crimean war, how can I find out if he was entitled to any medals?"

"Mrs Simpkins' children keep throwing their ball into my garden, what are you going to do about it?" and "Do your knickers match your uniform?" were about par for the course. Still it was interesting and helped keep her mind distracted from her own problems.

On the bus journey home, Sally again suggested calling on the skills of Uncle Mick.

"I know he's the guy who introduced you and Malcolm, but that's all I do know about him. He's not that long haired weirdo who keeps coming round trying to get us to flog his poetry pamphlets, is he?"

"Good grief no! That's mad Mike. Have you read his poetry?"

"No."

"Pornographic."

"Oh."

"And it doesn't rhyme. Malcolm's poetry always rhymes. I think it's just lazy if it doesn't rhyme."

"Well there are probably not many words which rhyme with bondage."

"Thought you hadn't read it."

"Haven't, I was just using my imagination."

"Well don't," Sally said.

"Sorry. So tell me about Uncle Mick."

"He's the animal welfare inspector."

"Oh yeah, I know who you mean. Is he Irish?" Lucy asked.

"His name is Mick O'Flaherty, and he greets everyone with 'top o' the morning to ya.' Polish obviously."

"That's it, I'm off."

"Hey, I was just kidding. Can't you take a joke?"

"My stop. See you tomorrow."

Lucy arrived at work later than Sally on Wednesday. She saw her talking to Mick O'Flaherty so kept out of sight, joining her friend once he'd gone.

"Oh, Lucy you just missed Uncle Mick, don't worry though I've told him all about you and he's on the case."

"Hang on a minute, what have you told him?"

"That you are a sad, lonely spinster in need of the services of a marriage broker, of course."

"A marriage what?"

"Oh don't worry about that, it's just an old Irish thing. Means that he's great at fixing people up."

"I don't need fixing up."

"Going to get a man on your own then?"

"Having a boyfriend is not the most important thing in the world you know. Haven't you heard of female emancipation?"

"You can still vote for goodness sake. I just want you to be as happy as I am with Malcolm."

"Yeah. I know you do, but I'm fine, really I am and I don't

need some weird bloke I don't know fixing me up with some other weird bloke I don't know."

"Suit yourself. You'd better tell Uncle Mick he's off the case. He works fast you know."

It was not until Friday that Mick O'Flaherty called into the council offices to double check if any more cases of animal neglect had been reported. Lucy spotted him and rushed out, saying she was taking her lunch break early.

"Mr O'Flaherty, may I have a word with you?"

"Ah. Lovely Lucy, top o' the morning to ya. Call me Uncle Mick, that's what all the girls I help call me."

"Mr O'Fla, um, Mick …oh. That's what I wish to discuss."

"My, but you're an impatient one."

"I beg your pardon."

"Oh, there's no need to beg."

"You don't understand."

"Ah to be sure I do. Was I not single myself once?"

"I'm quite sure you were; that's not the point."

"No of course not. It's you that's looking for a man now, not my lovely wife."

"I don't want a man!"

"You don't?"

"No."

"Now there's a thing. Well, aren't I broad minded then? Not to worry, I'll find you a girl." He winked, grinned and chuckled then left before the startled Lucy could react, let alone think of a reply. She ran after him and tried to explain. She wasn't sure she succeeded. Lucy herself was rather confused by the end of the conversation. She finally agreed to meet him at the animal rescue centre Saturday morning. He thought he had an answer to all her problems. Lucy hadn't known she had problems and, although she loved dogs, wasn't sure a puppy could solve them even if she did. That didn't deter Mr. O'Flaherty in his mission to set her up with at least a canine companion.

Lucy told her mother about the day's events, cautiously mentioning the fact she was to look at some homeless dogs. To her surprise the idea of a dog was accepted readily.

"I always had a dog before I met your father, but with his asthma we didn't have one after we married." She looked sadly at her husband's photograph in its silver frame. "Between us we could manage one, I'm sure. It'd be company for me when you're at work."

Lucy and her mother met Mick O'Flaherty and chose a mongrel pup. He had the ears of an Alsatian, the body of a terrier and a huge fuzzy tail. He was black with white spots, a negative of a Dalmatian. He was like no other dog, anywhere, ever. Time was given for Lucy to purchase a bed and other essentials before the visit to ensure that she and her mother would be able to provide a good home him.

As the time for Stripey to come and live with her neared, Lucy had many conversations with Mr. O'Flaherty. They were mostly about the dog.

"You'll be wanting sensible shoes to go walking him in."

Sensible shoes? Was he still thinking she'd prefer a girlfriend to a boyfriend? Looking down at her red patent stilettos and up at his innocent smile she decided he was just being practical. When he told her about interesting, yet muddy, paths which were ideal for dog walking she was sure she was right.

Mick had more practical advice, including the address of

a charity shop which saved donated towels and blankets, found to be in poor condition, for pet owners.

"Let you have them for loose change and they're easier to keep clean than them fancy pet beds as you can just swap them over when they get grubby."

"That's a good idea, thank you."

A few days before she was due to collect her new pet, Mick asked, "What are you going to call him?"

"I thought … Stripey."

Mick grinned. "That's just grand!"

"I don't think anything too sensible would suit him."

"To be sure you're right enough there. A name has to fit, that's why I like people to call me Uncle Mick."

Lucy resolved to address him that way in future. He was such a nice man, now she'd got to know him properly and he was no longer trying to fix her up with a partner of either sex, that she thought it would come easily.

On Uncle Mick's advice she enrolled herself and Stripey in puppy training classes. Conveniently the class began at the local village hall two days after Stripey officially became her dog. As she walked to the hall Lucy was astounded to see another dog almost identical to her own. They must be related.

She was impressed with his owner too. He was slim, but not weedy looking. Neatly dressed, clean shaven with his dark curly hair well cut. He looked just the sort of boy her mother would like her to bring home. Mum, Lucy had always felt, had excellent taste. He didn't hide the fact he'd noticed her too. His smile was relaxed and confident, that spark of attraction she'd been searching for sparkled in his eyes.

She introduced herself to him as they registered for the class. "Hi, I'm Lucy and this is Stripey."

"Patrick and er, Mickrick," he said in a soft drawl.

They discovered both dogs had come from the same rescue centre.

"They must be from the same litter," Lucy said.

"I can't see how it could be otherwise," Patrick agreed.

"It's great they've been reunited at these classes."

"It is, yes. I'm really glad I took the advice to sign up."

"Me too."

Lucy almost asked him if it had been a Mr O'Flaherty who'd made the suggestion. He'd been keen to see the puppies found good homes so it seemed entirely possible. Remembering Uncle Mick's reputation as a matchmaker made her reluctant to raise the subject; she didn't want Patrick to assume she needed such a service or thought he must.

Stripey responded well to the class and seemed eager to listen to his new mistress. He was even more eager to play with Mickrick though; the only times he didn't pay attention to Lucy was when he caught sight of his brother.

After the class finished, Lucy suggested she and Patrick allow the dogs to play together. "That's if you're not in a hurry to get off."

"I'm not, no."

The two puppies rolled each other over and over in a blur of black and white fur and fuzzy tails.

"Do you live close by?" Patrick asked. "If you do, maybe we could walk these two together sometimes."

"I live just up the road and walking them together is a

nice idea. I'm sure they'd like that." She could have added she rather thought she would too.

They exchanged phone numbers and arranged to meet the following evening.

Soon they were meeting regularly, discovering new paths and parks and talking about their dogs' progress.

At work too Stripey and his brother were an important part of Lucy's conversation.

"Yes but what about Patrick? Has he asked you out yet?" Sally asked.

"He's fine, but it's not like that, we're just good mates."

"Yeah, so why do you go on about him just slightly more than I do about my Malc then?"

It turned out that Sally was right and Lucy was wrong.

When they met with the dogs after work that evening, Patrick said, "Would you like to have dinner with me one evening?"

"Bring a picnic on our walk do you mean?"

"We could do that if you like, but I meant just the two of us in a restaurant."

"Like … a date?"

"Exactly like that, yes."

"Yes please."

They shared a huge pizza topped with Lucy's favourite vegetables, palma ham and mascarpone cheese as those were Patrick's preferred choices too. They drank prosecco from glasses which sparkled in the candlelight. Patrick held her hand as he walked her home. When he kissed her goodnight her heart beat faster than it had when she and Stripey had raced him and Mickrick up a hill.

On Saturday they look the dogs out for a long walk all morning, then sat on a blanket in the sun to share a picnic lunch. It felt so right to lie in his arms with the two dogs sprawled across them. On Sunday Patrick joined Lucy and her mother for lunch. Over the next few weeks they spent increasingly more time together until they, and their dogs, were hardly ever apart.

Lucy was so deeply affected by her happy relationship that she even sighed over the beautiful sentiments in Malcolm's wonderful poetry. Lucy was so happy with Patrick that even the most cynical and least romantic of her friends didn't doubt her future happiness. Lucy and Patrick were perfectly compatible in every way, including their ready made canine family.

One day when they were walking along the edge of a river, Lucy noticed something on Mickrick's collar which sparkled even more brightly than the sun on the water. "Oh that's really pretty."

"I'm glad you think so, it's for you," Patrick said.

Lucy knelt for a closer look. It was a diamond ring.

"I know it's supposed to be me on one knee, but Lucy, will you marry me?"

It took her a moment before she was able to stand, but when she did she hugged Patrick. "I will! Most definitely I will."

It was no surprise to Sally, Mick O'Flaherty or casual acquaintances when Lucy announced she and Patrick were engaged.

"I just knew you two would end up like me and Malc," Sally said.

"Ah to be sure, I recognised that look on your face.

Haven't I see it so many times before then?"

Mum was delighted. "Your dad would have been so pleased and I know he'd have liked Patrick."

"Thanks, Mum."

"He put some money aside for your wedding, so don't you worry about that. I don't want to wait long for a celebration though, how about having an engagement party?"

They decided to hold it in the same village hall which had been home to the puppy training classes. Sally helped with the arrangements and invited some people from work. Everyone brought a plate of food and a bottle or two for the buffet. Malcolm read a poem about the couple and Stripey and Mickrick. It was both funny and touching. It rhymed of course.

Lucy spotted Patrick bringing Mick O'Flaherty towards her. "It was nice of you to come, in a funny way I suppose I should be grateful to you. It was partly your idea about Stripey."

"Lucy," asked Patrick. "Do you two know each other then?"

"Yes to be sure we do, but don't worry 'bout it Patrick lad, go ahead and introduce us properly."

"Well, Mick I would like to present to you my darling fiancée Lucy. Lucy, meet my Uncle Mick."

7. A Glimmer Of Light

"Any idea where you'd like to go on holiday?" Kevin asked. He had to. If he didn't let his wife have a say in their plans he'd never hear the end of it. Some other men might plan a surprise trip, but that was a risk Kevin wasn't prepared to take.

"I'd like to go and see the northern lights," Angie said.

"*Stargazing Live* has a lot to answer for," he grumbled. Kevin, who faintly resembled Dara O'Briain especially in lack of hair, wasn't a fan. It wasn't so much the programme he objected to, as one of the presenters. Kevin's achievements were always being unfavourably compared with those of former classmate Brian Cox. Kevin had lost count of the number of times he'd had it pointed out that only one of them was now an internationally respected celebrity who could afford to whisk his wife away on exotic trips. Only one was still slim. Jealousy wasn't an attractive trait though, so Kevin tried not to show it and instead said, "Still if it's good enough for Brian, then maybe it'll be good enough for me."

Angie looked up. "The programme might have reminded me, but it didn't put the idea in my head. It's something I've always wanted to see."

"Is that really what you want to do on holiday? Look for the Northern Lights?"

"Yes, it'd be fun wouldn't it, to try?"

"I suppose, but they did say on the TV it was hard to predict where they'd be and you had to be really lucky to see them." He didn't want Angie to be disappointed and not just because it would be more ammunition against him.

"I know, but that doesn't mean we won't. After all you're really lucky."

"I am?"

"Married me didn't you?" She winked.

That was true. Angie was an attractive woman with may good points. "Hmmm. Oh, all right then. I'll look at holidays to Scandinavia. Don't suppose you'll want to camp there though?" He smiled bravely in an attempt to disguise his hope that she would.

"No, I wouldn't."

Kevin loved camping, a fact well known to his wife. That's why they'd spent their honeymoon under canvas, and every holiday since. Sometimes it had been their own two man job, on a few occasions they'd hired one of those posh ones which were ready erected on camp sites in France and Spain. So far they'd always done what he wanted for their holidays. Although he'd often been told that he always put himself first it hadn't actually occurred to him before that, when it came to holiday destinations, this was true. No wonder he was accused of being selfish. Well, not this time. He'd let Angie pick the hotel and he'd work overtime to pay for it. That might stop the complaints for a bit.

"Sorry, what did you say, love?" Ooops, not listening was another of the faults he'd been reminded of more than once.

"I said, how about Scotland? Although really I mean one of the islands. Didn't you say there was one of them you'd like to explore?" Angie asked.

"I did and I would, but we'd have a bit better chance of seeing the lights in Norway."

"Maybe, but like you say it's not guaranteed, so we should go somewhere we want to see anyway. That way if we miss the lights, we won't feel we wasted our time."

Naturally Kevin was easily persuaded. He did his best to ignore the months of little digs leading up to the trip. They didn't stop even when he bought Angie a pair of walking boots and a nice new waterproof jacket, but Kevin knew she'd be glad of them on the trip.

They walked for miles over dramatic rugged landscapes, stopping frequently to admire the scenery and get their breath back. Kevin captured photographs of several different bird species he'd never before seen in the wild. There was no sign of the Northern Lights though. Nor was there a single moan, gripe, complaint, nag or suggestion Kevin was in anyway inadequate. Well, not until the last night.

They camped fairly close to the airport to be sure not to miss the early flight home, which meant they once again had a mobile phone signal. The second Kevin answered the call he wished he hadn't.

"You've been ignoring me all week!" his mother screeched.

"Mum, I haven't …"

"Not that you'd listen to me anyway. I told you that trip was a mistake, but you insisted on going, and dragging that poor wife of yours along with you. I suppose she'll divorce you and that'll just be more humiliation for me."

He didn't hear the rest as Angie had reached over and switched off the phone.

She hugged him. "Don't listen to her, love. She's wrong about this trip, you know she is."

"Yes, you really did say you wanted to come."

"Exactly. And it's not the only thing she's wrong about. You're not a failure, not in any way and certainly not as a husband."

"Really?"

"Of course not, silly. Now come to bed and prove me right."

Hours later Angie shook him awake. "The light, Kevin. Come out and see."

Dutifully he pulled on his shorts and crawled out of the tent. In the East he saw a faint violet glow.

"Look at that! The Northern Lights! Told you we were lucky, didn't I?"

"No, you said I was, and you're right about that." Kevin looked at the lighter patch of sky that was almost certainly just light pollution and thought how lucky he was to have a wife who was so easily pleased. That more than made up for a mother who never would be.

8. True Romance

"Good weekend?" I asked young Rose, not expecting anything more exciting than the latest news about her mother and the cats.

"Wonderful, thank you, Sandy. I went camping with Claud. He's a fireman and a real outdoorsy type. We climbed a mountain for the clear air and the wonderful views. Then went swimming in a lake." She giggled. "We didn't have any swimming costumes so we were … uh, you know …"

"You went skinny dipping?"

"Yes." She blushed. "It was OK when we were actually swimming but boy was it cold when we got out! We were hungry too so we lit a fire and cooked fish we'd caught earlier and wrapped in wild garlic leaves. They were delicious!"

I'm pretty sure my mouth was hanging open by the end. It was the longest speech I'd ever heard her make. Usually she gets in a dither about leaving her mother alone when she works late and her idea of an adventurous meal is to have pickle in her lunchtime cheese sandwich. As for an action man boyfriend, it really didn't seem likely. And skinny dipping? I'd never seen her with the top button of her blouse undone, even in the height of summer.

I looked at her more closely. There was a healthy blush to her cheeks and her eyes sparkled.

"Sounds like fun," I said.

"Oh it was! I wasn't sure at first I'd be comfortable with someone so … rugged, I suppose is the word."

"But you were?" I prompted.

"Once I'd discovered the truth about the accident, I was. He's so considerate. He carried all our gear in a massive backpack so I was able to keep up with him, just about. And he has a vulnerable side. You should have seen his face when he thought of those poor little children and what people said about that."

Of course I wanted to know what people said about the children and if that were connected with the accident Rose referred to, but I didn't get the chance. One of the girls who runs our conferences phoned in sick and I had to rush off to Bath for a week. Later I asked Rose about her boyfriend.

"Carl is fine," she told me, though she didn't sound as though she cared. "Would be, wouldn't he? Thinks he's above everyone else and doesn't care about people except as patients."

"Carl?"

"Yeah, Carl the Snarl. He has to be the most obnoxious surgeon at St Mary's."

"Right," I muttered, wondering why she went out with him if that's what she thought and where St Mary's was. I'd not heard of a local hospital with that name.

"Brilliant of course, which partly justifies his arrogance. He can be charming if he wants to and he's so good looking and fit." Her sigh as she said the last bit answered my first question at least.

"But what about Claud?"

"Finished."

"That's a shame."

"Not at all. There are so many more, Sandy."

At that crucial point my boss informed me I'd have to spend the day in Sheffield with another colleague. On the journey I raised the puzzling subject of Rose and her boyfriends.

"Weird isn't it?" Laura said. "I mean she's not hideous or anything, but you wouldn't expect her to attract a hunky fireman and then dump him for a celebrated viola player would you?"

"Carl the Snarl plays the viola?"

"Who?"

I explained about the brilliant surgeon and asked, "Do you think she's making it all up?"

"I did wonder. Have you heard of Gregory Menzell?"

"No, but I haven't heard of any viola players except Yehudi Menuhin."

"He's a violin player," Laura corrected me.

"There's a difference?"

"According to Rose there is."

The day after I returned from my trip to Sheffield, I bumped into Rose and asked how she was getting on with Carl.

"Sandy, I feel dreadful."

"Oh dear, has he split up with you?" I asked, really wondering if she'd callously dumped him and moved onto the next already.

"No, I feel awful about the way I misjudged him. I've just found out about his parents. What a terrible tragedy," she broke off to wipe away tears. "No wonder he can't allow himself to identify emotionally with his patients and has to distance ..."

She was too distressed to explain properly so I patted her shoulder and suggested she get herself a cup of tea.

A few days later we learned the girl who'd gone sick just before each conference was in fact pregnant and suffering terrible morning sickness so I worked with Laura quite a bit over the next few weeks. We compared notes on Rose's love life.

"She has to be making it all up," Laura insisted. "The last one was a racing driver who took her to St Moritz for a week. She's got a sick mother and millions of cats, so who looks after them while she's away?"

"There are only three cats, but it does seem strange," I said. I didn't remember her having taken a week's leave but I'd been so busy I could have lost track. For all I knew the frail mother and cats she'd been telling me about for the last two years were the real fantasy.

"And what about that chef? Luigi was it? She ate so many pizzas and pasta dishes and rich desserts I almost went off Italian food hearing about it, yet she's still stick thin."

Rose isn't so terribly thin, but certainly slimmer than you'd expect from someone who's taken out for lavish meals several times a week and who's recently dated a chocolatier.

"She describes these men in great detail and they all sound very real."

"True," Laura agreed. "But if each one is as marvellous as she says, how come she quickly loses interest in them and moves onto the next?"

"I know. That doesn't sound like the nice considerate girl I've always thought she was."

"It just doesn't add up. Anyway, where on earth does she meet them all?"

I nodded. Although I didn't like to think Rose had become a serial liar, that seemed more likely than her suddenly becoming simultaneously irresistible to men and completely shallow and heartless.

When yet another conference coincided with Laura's holiday I decided it was the perfect opportunity to learn the truth about Rose and asked her to accompany me to Plymouth. Rose made arrangements for neighbours to keep an eye on her mother and look after the cats, but that seemed to involve far more fuss for two nights than had been the case for any of her trips away with boyfriends. By then I'd remembered seeing photos of the cats and speaking to the mother on the phone once and was sure then that Rose had been lying about the men. I gave her a chance to come clean.

"Won't you miss your boyfriend, that is if you have one at the moment?"

"Not at all; I'll bring him with me. I can bring one for you as well if you like?"

"Rose! I'm happily married and this is a work trip. I can't book an extra room …" I trailed off as it occurred to me that someone who got through men like she did wasn't likely to want a single room.

She just smiled and told me not to worry.

Of course I did worry until she turned up for the trip without a man. Instead she had an armful of books: romances.

"You can borrow as many as you like," she assured me.

I flicked through a couple and soon learnt where she'd

met Claude, Carl, Luigi and all the others. Then I saw her chuckle.

"Sorry, I know I talked about them as though they were real, but to me they sort of are and …" she blushed. "It was fun to tease you. Sorry."

"All right, I'll let you off," I said. "Reading them has certainly brought a smile to your face and a sparkle to your eye. But, Rose you shouldn't rely on books alone for romance. They're fine for a bit of fun and escapism, but you need to get out in the real world. You'll never meet a man this way."

"Actually I have. His name's Jimmy and he works in the bookshop. I read quickly but only buy one at a time so I have to go in quite frequently and we usually chat a bit."

I grinned. There was no 'have to' about it, Rose deliberately went in as often as she could because she liked the look of this boy, I was sure.

"I went in yesterday and bought two, explaining it was because I was going away with you, Sandy. He thought you were a man and asked if I was your boyfriend. When I said I didn't have one, he asked if I'd go out with him when I get back."

I don't know if they'll live happily ever after, but I'm looking forward to hearing much more about that particular story.

9. A Pain In The Heart

My name is Roger Garland and I'm dying. I'd expected my life to flash before my eyes. That's what's supposed to happen isn't it? Well it isn't happening to me. All I can see is Suzy's face. She looks concerned, but then she's always concerned about something.

The pain in my heart is terrible; it nearly masks that other pain, the one in my arm. I know what that means, a heart attack. I wonder if I'll die right away, like my Dad, or if I'll be kept alive on a machine so the family can say their goodbyes. I don't want that. Better to get it over with. The pain is subsiding, is that a good thing? Or does it mean my heart's given up the struggle?

The ambulance crew arrive and start fussing. They seem to be saying I'm not having a heart attack, but they'll take me to hospital. Silly idiots, am I dying or not? They lug me into the ambulance. I'm wired up to some sort of machine.

"Just to keep an eye on things, Roger," one of them says.

They ask a lot of fool questions but they don't bother with the siren. Maybe I'm not going to die just yet then.

On the journey, I remember the cause of my problem. Suzy. It's all Suzy's fault. Played football for the Red Lion, didn't I? She's been nagging something chronic about my health lately, had to do something to prove I'm not past it. Didn't work like I planned though. Ten minutes in I'm lying on the ground and the goalie is dialling 999.

Things had been fine until I took early retirement. Suzy had been a lovely bride, a wonderful wife, tremendous mother. We'd been happy in the beginning, despite the shortage of money, as I built up the business. Garland's Gardens has become successful. I decided three years ago, just after my fiftieth birthday, that the time had come to take things easier. Didn't want to be like my dad and not live long enough to retire. My sons took over the business. No more digging, no more carrying stuff, no more coming home exhausted.

At first, Suzy was happy too. We'd started going out for meals regularly, and popping down the pub most lunchtimes. We both put on a bit of weight. That's only natural at our age. Suzy said we should take some exercise and eat healthily. I wasn't having any of that. Suzy joined a gym, I asked her to drop me off at the pub on her way and pick me up afterwards.

"You could walk there, Roger if you must go. It's less than a mile."

Yes, that was probably when the nagging started. A right pain in the… well a pain is what she became.

She started feeding me salad or steamed fish for my dinner. I wanted proper food. She'd made pies and hot pots and roasts before. That was the kind of food I still wanted. We ate out more. I got to eat what I wanted, but not in peace.

"Why don't you have a jacket potato and green salad with that?" she'd ask.

Because I wanted chips, onion rings, creamy sauce and battered mushrooms, that was why. I've worked hard in order to afford the good things in life. Why was she so set on us not enjoying the odd luxury? She didn't like my cigars either. Patches, that's what she thought I should have.

I'd shown her that article in the paper, about how alcohol was good for you. She'd not even read it when she started on that red wine and scotch weren't the same thing. Said a glass of one was not the same as double shot after double shot of the other. Then she'd found some article in her magazine about eating five portions of fruit and vegetables a day. Five! And yet she wants me to cut back on what I eat. You can't trust what these scientists tell you anyway, what's good for you one day will kill you the next.

When your time's up, it's up. My dad died when he was the age I am now. His heart packed up, no reason at all. He was at the bar with his mates, same as always, then wallop. Stands to reason I'll be the same. No point in worrying. Suzy doesn't like me talking like that. She says if I look after myself, there's no reason I can't live for years.

"Don't you want to see your grandchildren?" she asked when I refused to go to the doctors for all them tests.

Of course, I'd like to see my grandchildren. The first is due in four months time. I'd hoped to still be around for the birth. Secretly I'd wanted to see them all born, hoped there'd be a few. I wanted to play with them in the park, watch them start school. I still want that, only now it's too late.

At hospital, there are more tests, silly questions over and over. They talk at me, but I don't listen. Truth is I don't want to hear what they have to say. Then Suzy is with me.

"Oh, Roger my love, I thought you were going to die."

"Me too. Am I not going to then?"

"No, not if you're sensible. Haven't you been listening to the doctors?"

"Some of it. Get some exercise they said. Don't they

know that's what got me here? A heart attack because of too much exercise."

"Not a heart attack, Roger, Angina. That's because you suddenly started racing around on a football pitch. Gentle exercise will help, but you've got to be sensible."

Sensible, that's what everyone keeps saying. A sensible diet, moderate exercise, cut down on the drink, quit the smoking. Sensible doesn't sound much fun.

Suzy takes me home from hospital and I agree to try, for her sake. I keep the doctor's appointment that the hospital recommended. Turns out she wasn't just nagging for the sake of it. She was trying to help, because she loves me. She doesn't want her family to loose their father, me, too early. Turns out that most of what she said was right and if I behave sensibly, I will get to see my grandkids.

Sensible, that word again. I'm beginning to see that it isn't so stupid, it is, well, sensible.

The doctor suggests I give up smoking. "I can prescribe patches if you like."

To her credit Suzy doesn't so much as smile at that. She takes me home. I don't want to read all the leaflets the doctor gave me, I want to get on and enjoy my life. Better be careful how I put that to Suzy though.

"Let's go down the pub, " I suggest.

"Do you think that's sensible?"

"Yes, I do. We'll walk down there. It might take a while, but there's no rush. Someone said they do a nice salmon salad, I think I'll try that for dinner tonight."

My name is Roger Garland, I can be a bit of a pain to my wife, but I'm lucky that she still loves me as much as I love her. We're going to live long and happy lives.

10. Too Good To Be True

Dear freind,

i am contacting you because i have $600,000 (six hundred thousand american dollars) that i need to pay into an account outside Nigeria. this is absolutely legal and NOT a scam. the money belongs to my family and as a reward for helping us, we would offer you 10 % (ten per cent) …

Beverley deleted the email scam. How did anyone ever fall for them? They were obviously too good to be true. Even little kids knew not to take sweets from strangers. Surely everyone knew anything that seemed unbelievable actually was?

"You worry too much," Mum had said more than once.

That wasn't true, not really. Beverley just liked to know all the possible catches before she did anything. It was easy to miss the disadvantages, as she knew only too well from her own experience. There was the time the school bully offered her chocolate as a peace offering. Pleased the boy seemed to have seen the error of his ways, she'd eaten the whole bar before she realised it wasn't regular chocolate, but the laxative kind. She'd once sent 'no money now' for the amazing investment in miniature cat ornaments. When the first cat and invoice arrived she'd calculated how much the entire collection would cost and made a shrewd guess about her chances of recouping the costs. At least Mum had liked the cat when Beverley gave it to her for Christmas.

Beverley chose the biscuits with 'buy one get one free'

offer until she realised it was her waist and not her savings increasing.

Richard was too good to be true. He was attractive, although not so handsome he was vain. He was good looking enough that when she first saw him she doubted he'd be interested in her. He reminded her of a boy who'd once asked her out for a bet when she was fifteen. It never happened again, because if a gorgeous guy she hardly knew spoke to her she'd be on the look out for the signs (not meeting her eyes, looking round to see who was watching them) and never gave him the chance to ask. She didn't give anyone a chance to trick her or make her look a fool.

Beverley met Richard through their respective jobs and had got to know him before he asked her out, so she'd been reasonably confident his offer of a meal was genuine.

"OK, but I'll meet you at the restaurant and get a taxi home."

"Sensible precaution. I'll see you at seven-thirty then?"

She'd soon learnt that everything about him was genuine. He had a job, didn't drink too much, didn't smoke, was nice to animals, her family liked him, his liked her. He laughed at her jokes, put the toilet seat down, knew that consolidating their loans into one easy payment wouldn't help them clear the mortgage any quicker and ... He was too good to be true.

He'd been patient when it took months for her to commit to moving in with him. She kept finding excuses to go back 'home' for a night and more of her clothes were in her parents' house than in the flat that was supposed to be theirs. When she'd looked down into his eyes as he knelt before her holding a ring box, he'd just nodded when she asked for more time.

"Why don't we take a short holiday? Just us. No pressure and I'll convince you how great I am."

She'd agreed to the holiday, although she doubted it would help. She already knew how great he was. What she wanted was to see the small print.

"You want your head examined, my girl," Mum had said when she'd shown her the ring she'd agreed to wear around her neck. "He's perfect for you. Get that ring on your finger where it belongs."

She couldn't – not until she was absolutely sure.

"Marry him before he changes his mind," her friends urged.

Beverley knew he wouldn't do that in a hurry. He wasn't fickle and he wasn't manipulative. As Mum said he was perfect: too good to be true.

"Perfect for you, not completely perfect. He's human and got faults the same as anyone else," Mum said.

"Really?" If that was true she could marry him without worrying she'd discover the catch once it was too late.

"Yes."

"Such as?" Beverley asked.

"I'm thinking. Oh, I know, he sometimes criticises your driving."

"Yes, but the last time was when I dented the car getting it out the garage and the time before was when I forgot to put the hand-brake on and it rolled into a ditch. Honesty isn't really a fault is it?"

"Well, he's not exactly spontaneous, is he? He plans everything in advance and won't commit to the simplest thing without asking dozens of questions first."

"I like that about him."

"Yes, I suppose you would."

Beverley drove home very carefully. Although Richard would be justified in claiming she was sometimes careless with the car, he'd never actually done so; he'd simply explained to Mum what happened after Beverley herself had raised the subject.

She parked the car without incident and rushed up to kiss Richard. He didn't seem as keen to see her as usual.

"What's up?" she asked.

"I'll make a cup of tea, shall I?" He didn't look her in the eye as he evaded the question. Something must be wrong.

"Are you ill?"

"No. And neither are any of my family or our friends, don't worry."

"Lost your job?" Beverley followed him into the kitchen.

"No, it's nothing really."

"Come on, tell me. You know I'll worry otherwise."

Richard filled the kettle and put tea bags into their mugs before answering. "It's just that I feel so stupid. I wanted to impress you with a nice holiday and not worry you with anything."

"Well you have. I admit I was a little concerned about whether we could afford it. But you got such a great deal."

"No, I didn't. You'll think I'm such an idiot. I checked the holiday company where properly registered and paid with my credit card so we'd be covered if anything went wrong and got insurance. I even checked the airport wasn't 60 miles from the resort."

"Yes, you're always sensible and …"

"I didn't check they'd actually built the hotel. Someone at work told me about one of these Watchdog programmes on telly investigating cheap holidays so when I got home I checked. The place is still a building site. I think we'll get the money back, but it's …"

Beverley kissed him. "It doesn't matter."

"It does, it does. I know what you think about gullible idiots who fall for scams and …"

"Richard, it was just an honest mistake. At least you found out before we were stuck in an airport with nowhere to go and it does prove you're human."

"But I promised you a nice holiday and now …"

"I expect you've learnt your lesson."

"Oh yes, I'll read all the small print on any bookings I make in future and check out the destination on the internet."

"Good, then I'm sure you'll book us a great honeymoon."

Beverley took the ring off the chain and handed it to him. He dropped to one knee and slid the gold and diamond band onto her finger. It was slightly too big and absolutely perfect.

11. Drawn By Adam

I was so desperate for Adam to notice me I actually asked the advice of the guys in despatch. First I sidled over to the edge of the conversation, hoping to pick up tips. As usual they were talking about football.

I knew that wasn't going to help me. I'd tried discussing it with Adam. It hadn't gone well. I'd repeated something I'd overheard about an amazing hat trick. Sadly, it had been scored against the team Adam supports.

I asked, "So boys, what interests you, apart from footie?"

"Well, Tracie, there are a couple of things," I was informed. More than one of them gazed at my chest.

"Is that all you lot think about?"

"Pretty much."

Some of them looked embarrassed, but none denied it.

"You're not really helping," I said.

"Well, what d'you want to know?"

"How can I get a man to notice me?"

"Wouldn't have thought you had much trouble," one of them said.

"I'll notice you as much as you like," another offered, still not looking at my face.

"Take your clothes off, he'll notice you then."

I'd stomped back to my desk. I didn't doubt their idea would work, but it wasn't exactly subtle and probably wouldn't create the reaction I wanted.

At lunchtime, I thought of another option. I sat at the same table as Adam and managed to bring up the subject of hobbies. I'd planned to reveal my interest in aromatherapy and hope he liked the idea of having his back rubbed. Before I could, he mentioned pottery evening classes. Instantly I thought of that sexy scene with Patrick Swayze, in *Ghost*.

I came out of my daydream and said, "I think I'd like to try."

"Try what, Tracie?"

"Pottery."

"I've got the details somewhere, I'll find them for you," Adam said.

Yes! I knew once he saw me away from work and out of my awful uniform, he'd be more interested in me.

"Oh, OK," I managed to say calmly. Well, I didn't want to scare the guy off.

An hour later, he gave me the course details. "It's a pity we won't be doing it together, it might have been fun."

I realised, thanks to Patrick Swayze, I'd missed a vital part of the lunchtime conversation.

Obviously, I couldn't tell Adam I hadn't been listening, so I made some tactful inquiries. I discovered pottery clashed with another course, and he'd signed up for whatever it was.

I rang the college. There were nine courses coinciding with pottery. At least I knew when he'd be there, all I had to do was hang about in reception and see where he went.

It wasn't as easy as that. I spotted him in the crowds of people registering and saw which exit he took from reception, but couldn't follow without being noticed.

Although I wanted to be noticed, of course, I didn't want him thinking of me as a crazy stalker. I went back the next week, feeling even more like a stalker, but trying to convince myself I was just curious. Perhaps I'd begun to get just a little obsessed by that stage, but I was sure if Adam could see me as something other than a work colleague, the rest would be easy. My plan nearly failed again. I arrived just in time to see Adam walk towards a stairway. Racing to the top I saw him enter a classroom, so waited outside for a minute, listening. Just as I was sure he was alone, I heard people on the stairs, so dived into the room opposite. The couple went straight by, but more were coming. By the time I felt it was safe to leave my hiding place, I wasn't sure Adam was still on his own. I left and bumped into someone on the stairs.

"Tracie?"

"Miss Birch?"

"Call me Sara, I'm not your form tutor now. What are you doing lurking in corridors?"

I don't know why, but I told her everything.

"So what were you planning to do, follow him into the classroom and throw off your clothes? I think you need to be a little more subtle. I have an idea."

Of course, she was right, but her plan was still pretty close to the suggestion of the boys at work.

We discussed the best date and way to do it, deciding I should get to the classroom first and be ready before Adam arrived. We couldn't be sure he would be on his own for long. There was another reason for getting prepared, the issue of bra straps, zips and buttons. Some people might be able to effortlessly remove their clothes in front of an audience, but I wasn't sure I could. Struggling to undo fastenings and remove clothing wouldn't look alluring. Really, the best thing would be for me to get there early, get undressed behind the notice board, slip into a robe and wait for the right moment to reveal my charms.

For once, everything went as planned. I didn't have an unsightly rash, I wasn't feeling bloated and the weather wasn't too cold. As I stepped into view, letting my robe fall to my feet, it was obvious Adam had noticed me. His mouth fell open and he stared. I thought for a moment I'd made a mistake, but then he smiled, fidgeted in his chair and began to pay me some real interest. He was very thorough, a true artist. My lips, my thighs, my breasts all received the same slow, gentle attention. His hands followed the swell of my hips, methodically his fingers worked over every contour of my body.

"You must be cold," a voice murmured.

It would have been perfect, except it wasn't Adam handing me my robe. It was Sara Birch. She'd hired me as the model for life drawing classes.

I went behind the screen to dress.

"I feel such an idiot," I said. "Adam might have noticed me, but he's still not interested. All I've done is to get myself freezing cold."

Fully dressed, I once again emerged from behind the screen and into the classroom. Sara had gone. Only Adam remained.

"Actually, I am interested. Want to come for a drink to warm you up?"

12. I Wonder Who It's From?

Mum held the envelope to the light and peered at the postmark. "I wonder who this could be from?"

Why the drama whenever she gets a letter? She checks handwriting, postmark, even looks for a return address.

"Just open it, Mum."

"I can't. It's not mine." She slid it across the table.

It was addressed to me. I picked up the cream coloured envelope. It felt like a card; who could it be from? Before I ripped it open, I just happened to notice the postmark was local. Inside was a Valentine's card; the second one I'd ever received. Last year I got one from Dad. It was a funny one, but made me sad. Dad hadn't attempted to disguise his writing and had sent it because he knew I wouldn't be getting one from anyone else.

This year's card was a sweet, romantic one. The handwriting wasn't Dad's and it had been posted, not just 'appeared' on the hall table on Valentine's Day. It was four days early; Dad's a last minute kind of guy. 'To sweet Julie', it read and was signed, 'a secret admirer'. Of course it was, however much I hoped, there was fat chance of my getting a card signed by Gary.

I didn't have time to figure out who sent it. Instead, I ran upstairs and changed my baggy Jeans and trainers for a skirt and decent shoes. I took the elastic band off my hair and gave it a good brushing then slicked on some lip-gloss.

Although I didn't have a clue who'd sent the card, the chances were it was someone from college. I didn't go anywhere else. Whoever it was, I didn't want him thinking he'd made a mistake.

The bus journey didn't reveal any likely candidates. There were a couple of lads, but there was no way they'd know my address. Besides, nobody had ever made any effort to sit near me, or talk. I shook my head, that wasn't a clue. If I liked a bloke, I didn't show it. I was too shy to speak first, even to Gary.

My guess was the sender of the card was shy too. Why else would I get an anonymous and unexpected Valentine's card? Whoever it was, probably felt pretty nervous that morning. Even if it was someone I'd never be interested in, I was pleased to be admired. I'd reward him with a charming smile.

I started grinning like my future love life depended on it, which it probably did. I grinned at the old guy on reception, I grinned at every bloke I passed on the way to class and I was preparing to grin at my tutor as I went in. Mr Rogers wasn't there; Gary was. I grinned at him and wonder of wonders he smiled back. Result!

Gary was always early to class, which is why I'd started getting the earlier bus in. We didn't speak or anything, I didn't have the nerve for that, but occasionally he nodded at me and I'd nod back. It felt good just to be alone with him for a few minutes and know he was aware of me. Thinking of Gary being early in gave me this crazy idea. If he sent a card, he'd probably get it in the post early. It couldn't have been him though – could it?

Tuesday morning there was no card, but that didn't matter, if the first one was from Gary, then one was enough.

"You look nice, Julie," Dad said.

I grinned at him, my face was getting used to that expression. I'd conditioned my hair, used my lip-gloss again as well as some mascara and ironed a blouse and skirt instead of pulling on jeans and a jumper. It was good to hear the effort was worth it.

Gary was in the classroom again when I arrived. He nodded.

"Morning," I managed to say.

He smiled at me, "Morning, Julie."

Yes!

On Wednesday, there was no card and no compliment from Dad. That didn't matter; I knew I looked as good as I was ever likely to. Gary seemed to think so anyway.

He said, "Hello," as I arrived. When I returned his greeting, he came and sat on the edge of my desk to chat. Nothing special, just about our homework, but at least we were talking.

Thursday was even better. I'd put my hair up and he told me it looked good. Amazingly I didn't go to pieces. I suppose I figured that if I could handle the guy sending me a Valentine's card, I could handle a compliment.

"You're not looking so bad yourself, Gaz," I said. I was practically flirting with him.

Friday was when I got the shock. The card on Monday was a surprise; the lack of one on Valentine's Day was a shock.

"Where's my card, Dad? Don't you love me any more?"

"Of course I do," he said and gave me a hug. "Your mum said you'd worked out who sent Monday's card."

I had, but it turned out I'd worked it out wrong. It had been from Dad. He'd done that trick of writing with the other hand to disguise his writing and posted it early so he didn't forget.

My breakfast lost its appeal. I'd made a complete fool of myself with Gary. He'd not sent me a card, probably wasn't the slightest bit interested and I'd … Well, all I'd really done was talk to the guy. Maybe it wasn't a complete disaster. I could just go back to catching the later bus and avoid any embarrassing early morning meetings.

That's what I did. I got the later bus and walked into class after nearly everybody else had arrived. On my desk was a bright pink envelope.

Who could it be from? I ripped it open. The signature was nothing more than a question mark. I glanced at Gary, he was grinning at me and his face was the same bright pink as the envelope.

13. Just This One Time

Whether it was her husband Brian's assumption she'd redecorate the lounge during her week off, or her colleague Steve's sympathy at the near impossibility of doing so, she couldn't say, but Sally had agreed to have a drink with Steve one lunchtime.

He was so understanding. "I know kids can be hard work. I don't know how you manage to care for them, be reliable at work, and still look so amazing."

Everyone else thought she was lucky to get 'yet another' week off work. They didn't realise that when you have three children the half term isn't exactly a holiday. Even Sally's husband hadn't got a clue, or pretended he hadn't. As her job at the school was 'only' part time Brian assumed she could easily work, look after the children and still be the perfect wife who'd greet him neatly made-up, with dinner cooking and the next day's shirt nicely ironed every evening.

The hour she spent in Steve's company really cheered her up and when he suggested they meet again she'd been tempted.

"I don't think that would be a good idea," she'd said, not very convincingly.

He'd given her a 'can't blame a guy for trying' smile and shrug. "Well you've got my number. Call me anytime you want to talk … or whatever."

Sally told herself she couldn't meet Steve outside of work

again. Well, probably couldn't and definitely shouldn't.

Although by Friday she was starting to feel as though she could and that for the sake of her sanity maybe she should. On Monday Brian had seemed surprised the children were still up.

"Shall I put them to bed while you sort out dinner?" he offered half heartedly.

"No, you've been working all day," she pointed out.

"OK then." Naturally it didn't occur to him she'd had a tiring day.

"Sorry it's late," she said when dinner was ready at last.

"That's OK. I can see you've been busy." He gestured towards the living room where the sofa and TV were covered with cloths to protect them from the sugar soap solution she'd used to wash down the walls.

It might not seem to him that she'd made much progress, but she'd like to see him do better with a baby and two children to keep amused.

On Tuesday dinner was on time. Brian said, "This pie looks good. Did you make it yourself?"

Sally ignored his sarcasm. It was rare for her to serve anything ready made, but she was tired.

On Wednesday Brian commented on the paint fumes as if she and her thumping head might not have noticed.

On Thursday he announced he was taking them all out for the day on Friday. "What with the decorating you've not had that much of a break this week and it'd be nice to spend some quality time with the children."

"Are you trying to say I neglect the children?" She bit back a retort that if he didn't spend half the weekend playing golf he'd see a lot more of his family.

"Of course not, Sally. I know you can do everything perfectly."

Steve had said something similar, but it had been a compliment coming from him. Brian made it an insult.

He must have seen something in her expression because he apologised. "I just thought it would be fun to take off for the day and do something different."

She forced a smile. She used to love his spontaneity. Before they had the children she occasionally came home on a Friday evening to find him stuffing clothes into a suitcase as he explained he'd got a great last minute deal on a weekend break, or he'd buy a food they'd never tried, or take her ice skating in her lunch break. None of that was possible now. Travelling with toddlers and babies required enormous preparation, fussy eating habits meant they stuck to a limited range of dishes and these days her lunch break involved eating a sandwich at two o'clock as she drove to collect the kids from the childminders.

The drive to Portsmouth was pleasant enough if rather noisy. Brian taught the children sea shanties which they happily repeated over and over. He fed them sweets too, ones he'd bought without a word to her. Sally told herself it wouldn't hurt just for that day, though she wished it wasn't always her who had to say 'no' in the supermarket and Brian who always got to be the one who provided the treats.

When Brian paid for the parking ticket Sally put the remaining sweets out of sight as she got Laura's push chair, and the carrier for Lucy, from the boot. The children hyper in the morning was one thing, she didn't want them having a sugar rush just as she was trying to get them settled that evening.

"What's that?" Tim asked, pointing.

"The Spinnaker Tower," Brian told him.

"What's it for?"

"People go up there to look at the view."

"Can we go? Please?"

"Maybe if there's time."

"Yay!"

"Yay!" Laura repeated his cry.

They bought their ticket for the Historic Dockyard.

Brian opened the map they'd been given. "Where shall we go first?"

"How about we start at the furthest point and work our way out?" Sally suggested.

"Good idea. That'd be … the Marie Rose."

Sally began to relax and enjoy herself. It was good to get away from the routine. On the way through the dockyard the children posed for pictures by ships' figureheads, anchors and a model pirate. Brian and Sally took it in turns to take the pictures or to be in them. She didn't have to fake her smile in a single one.

The children were excited to see a cross channel ferry go by and thrilled when they spotted HMS Victory.

"Pirate ship! Pirate ship!"

The Marie Rose exhibition was fascinating to the adults, but of less interest to their children who were eager to go onboard Victory.

"Maybe they're a bit young for this one," Brian conceded.

"They'll enjoy the ones they can get onto more," Sally reassured him. Visiting the Dockyard had been a good idea, she didn't want him to feel it wasn't.

Sally tried to persuade the children to visit the toilet before they boarded Victory.

"I wanna go on piwate ship now!" Laura insisted.

"Yay!" Tim added.

"The toilets are right here it won't take long."

"For goodness sake, Sally just relax will you? I'm sure they'll let us know if they want to go."

Sally bit her tongue and counted to ten before taking Laura out of her pushchair. Holding the toddler's hand and carrying the baby, she followed Tim and Brian up the gangway.

Brian transformed into a tour guide as soon as he stepped onto the ship. A loud tour guide.

"See how low the ceilings are, kids? That's because people used to be much shorter in the old days."

"Why did they, Daddy?" Tim asked.

"Um, it might have been what they ate."

"What food makes you shorter, Daddy?"

"It didn't make them shorter."

"You said it did."

"Bwussel spwouts make me fart," Laura informed the world.

"It wasn't what they eat, but what they didn't eat," Brian tried to explain.

"But you said …"

Sally turned to read a sign to hide her amusement. Conversations like that were normal for her, but Brian seemed to be floundering. Eventually he managed to change the subject by showing them the tools used to load the big cannons.

"They're called guns on a ship," Sally said. She'd just learned that from the sign.

"We see where piwates live?" Laura asked.

"OK, love. I think we need to go upstairs next."

"They're not called stairs on a ship," Brian told them. "They're ladders."

"Not going on ladder," Laura yelled.

"Come on, Laura," Brian said.

Laura screamed. "No!"

Brian grabbed her hand.

"No! No! No ladder!"

Gently Sally pulled Laura to her. "It's OK, love. We'll go up the stairs instead."

Instantly Laura calmed down. She climbed the wooden steps without fuss.

Brian led them into an area signposted as 'The Great Cabin'.

"Look kids, this is where the officers eat with the captain."

"Need toilet," Laura said.

"You'll have to wait," Brian said.

"Can't."

"Are we all going to go, or just me and Laura?" Sally asked.

"You take her," was Brian's predictable reply.

Sally unclipped Lucy's carrier and slipped it off her shoulders leaving Brian holding the baby.

By the time she returned with Laura, Brian and the others had moved on. Laura enjoyed the mad scramble round the different decks looking for them. Just after the family were reunited they came across a tour guide who explained what it would be like to live onboard. He was very good, making the children squeal as he told them about maggots in the biscuits and then laugh with his demonstration of walking about the low deck after drinking his rum ration. As he was at least six foot tall that involved plenty of contact between his head and the beams.

They were all ready for lunch by the time they'd finished exploring the ship. The onsite restaurant had a good range of cooked meals as well as pirate picnics for the little ones. It did take Laura and Tim a while to choose what they'd like, but not once did they come close to uttering the dreaded 'don't like that'. Sally got the children settled, lifted her own fork to her mouth and heard a wail from Laura.

"What's wrong, love?"

"Lost Teddy!"

"Where did you have him last?" Sally asked. There was just a chance the girl would remember.

"Dunno."

"He's on the pirate ship," Tim said. "He was having dinner at that shiny table, wasn't he, Dad?"

"Oh yes. We took his picture." Brian had the decency to look embarrassed. Or maybe that was just because of the fuss Laura was making.

"He'll be having a lovely lunch just like us," Sally said. "He'll like that."

"Be OK?"

"Yes he will. You eat your lunch and then we'll go and get him. Or perhaps just one of us?" she suggested to Brian.

"Good idea," Brain said. He continued to savour his food.

Sally gulped down hers. "I'll go get Teddy then."

Brian just nodded.

She ran back down to Victory and collected Teddy from a tour guide in the Great Cabin; a part of the ship she'd barely seen as she'd had to go off with Laura as soon as she got there. "Thank you so much."

"You're welcome. Have you got any questions about the ship while you're on your own? I know it can be difficult to stay too long in one place and ask when you have children with you."

"I did rather rush through," Sally admitted. "This is where the officers ate, wasn't it?" she asked, remembering Brian saying something similar.

"A lot of people think that, but actually this cabin was just for the admiral. He entertained in here while they were in port."

"Oh." Brian didn't know everything then. What else had he said? Oh yes. "What about people being shorter back then? Was it because of their food?"

"Actually people weren't really much shorter. It seems like they must have been because of the low decks, but that was to keep the ship stable."

"Seems I've been misinformed."

"Don't worry, a lot of people make the same mistake. It's not your fault you don't know. That's why we're here; to answer questions."

No it wasn't her fault, it was Brian's. He thought he knew everything and didn't bother to ask. No, that wasn't fair, he was trying to entertain the kids. Just as Sally was wondering how that was going her phone rang. Couldn't he even trust her to pick up the bear? Obviously he had no idea how often she'd had to do this with all the kids in tow.

Remembering phones were supposed to be off while on the ship she apologised, quickly hissed, "Can't talk now," and disconnected. "Well thanks again, I'd better go," she said to the guide.

"You're welcome and feel free to look around the parts of the ship you missed and ask the other guides if you have questions."

Before she could reply, Sally's mobile beeped indicating a text message.

"Sorry. I thought I'd switched it off." She made sure it was off but not before she'd read the text. 'Laura needs toilet again. Come back right away.'

Sally sighed. "Sadly I can't look round. I've been summonsed."

Sally wasn't sure how to get off the ship unless she followed the tour route so it seemed that she'd have to rush round it all again. Or she could do as the tour guide suggested and have a proper look at the bits she'd missed. It was because she'd had to take Laura to the toilet she'd not seen it the first time. Was it asking too much for Brian to take her just this once so she didn't miss her second opportunity?

Tempted though she was, Sally made her way to the exit as quickly as she could. Once she'd left the ship she switched her phone back on. There was another text from Brian and a frantic sounding voicemail message. There was also a text from Steve. 'Please call me when you can talk.'

She rang him and soon realised that it was him, not Brian, who'd called when she was on the ship.

"You won't be needed in work on Monday after all,"

Steve said. It was a teacher training day and Sally had been told she might have to go in for a meeting.

"Oh good, I can get the decorating finished."

"I have a better idea. We could go out somewhere interesting, stop for lunch in a quiet little pub, just get to know each other a bit."

Sally was tempted. A leisurely day out and a meal she could eat without interruptions sounded idyllic. It wouldn't be difficult to drop the children off as usual and meet him somewhere. No one would know.

"I have to go, Brian's waiting for me," she said then disconnected. She was aware she hadn't given him an answer.

When Sally reached her family she found Lucy crying, Tim and Laura sulking and Brian less than happy. "Where have you been? Laura couldn't wait for you. You've no idea how awkward it was. I couldn't leave the other two outside while I took Laura in and they didn't want to go in. "

"Actually, I do know. It happens every week in the supermarket while you're at golf."

"Oh, yes. I suppose so." Clearly that hadn't occurred to him before.

Steve had been right when he'd said Brian didn't really appreciate all she did. It wasn't entirely her husband's fault though. He didn't know how difficult it was organising the children as he'd never had to try. Even when she was in hospital giving birth, he had both their mothers looking after him and the other children. Afterwards she'd be so keen to resume the job she loved that she'd insisted she could cope with no more assistance than the services of a childminder while she was at work. She should have admitted she was finding it difficult to do everything. So difficult that she'd been persuaded to abandon her children, forget her husband and responsibilities to drink wine with Steve.

Sally couldn't stop the tears falling until Brian pulled her into his arms. "Talk to me, love."

"Sorry, I'll be all right in a minute." She wiped her face, blew her nose and tried to smile at her children who were staring at her.

"Are we ready to go on the boat trip?" Brian asked.

"Yay!" Laura and Tim brightened up immediately.

When Sally suggested she change Lucy, and Tim use the toilet, Brian took his son into the gents. Perhaps he had learned something.

After a tour round Portsmouth harbour in a boat they boarded HMS Warrior. That visit was accomplished without a hitch. The children sat quietly and listened as one of the guides there, who'd been a sailor himself, kept them entertained with stories about life at sea.

When they left the dockyard, Tim asked it they were going to go up the big tower.

"It's getting late," Sally said. "It'll be tea time soon."

Brian removed Laura from her push chair, pointed out a statue and told Tim and his sister to go and find out what it was. Then he again asked her to tell him what was wrong.

"Nothing."

"Yes there is. You don't cry over nothing. You're the most capable person I've ever met. You're fantastic with the kids, look after me, work, run the house. I knew all that of course, but I hadn't stopped to think how much was involved. You're superwoman."

"No. No I'm not. When will you see I just can't do everything perfectly all the time?"

"When will you see you don't have too? Not on your own."

Maybe he had a point. When they'd moved into the house they'd decorated it together after work. They'd eaten take-aways and spent time doing fun things together. They'd been a team then. Maybe they could be again.

Brian said, "I know you're not keen on the kids eating burgers or staying up late, but I was thinking we could stay here until a bit later then stop for a meal on the way home. It'd save you cooking tonight and arguments over bed time. Then we can relax over a glass of wine once they're asleep."

"I suppose once wouldn't hurt."

"And you'll actually sit down and drink it with me, not do the ironing or give the skirting boards a final coat of gloss?"

"All right. But if I don't do anything tonight, I'll have to do it tomorrow. That means you'll have to give up golf this week and help me paint, or mind the kids, or do the shopping."

"I suppose once wouldn't hurt."

"It'll have to be more than once, Brian. You don't have to give up golf, but I could really do with some regular help ..." She trailed off when she saw him grinning

"I think maybe I've lost superwoman and got my wife back."

"You'd better practice shopping with little ones in tow. Take the kids and buy tickets for the tower."

While he did, Sally sent a text to Steve. 'It's a no to Monday. I'll see you at work – and only at work.'

14. Mistletoe And Wine

Emily woke because of the tiny feet kicking just behind her left ear. Of course, it couldn't really be anything kicking her; she had no pets, the children were in their own rooms and, since the divorce, she slept alone. Perhaps she was lying on one of the children's toys? She sat up to look and saw what looked like a pixie at the bottom of her bed. The boys didn't have toy pixies. She felt the kicking again and twisted her head. The mirror on her dressing table showed another pixie clinging to her head, and he was moving.

Emily closed her eyes tight shut and lay back down. She hadn't had a drink for months so wasn't surprised that the couple she'd drunk last night had gone straight to her head. Still, it was only two glasses of mulled wine, sipped slowly over the course of a couple of hours. Surely, that wasn't enough to make her wake up with little people dancing on her?

"I'm not dancing. Why would I be dancing? There's too much work to do," the smallest little person said in a squeaky voice.

"Well you look like you're dancing," his diminutive companion squealed in reply.

Now she was hearing things. Marvellous. How could she have let herself get into this state? Since Dave left, she'd had sole charge of the children and, despite his claims to the contrary, she'd coped very well. Then for the first time in ages she'd left them in someone else's care. She'd gone to the office party, and apparently, got hopelessly drunk. What an idiot she'd been. Dave and that woman were trying for custody; Emily couldn't risk seeming irresponsible.

"Stop jigging around you loon, you're going to wake her up," the squealing voice muttered.

"Well it's not my fault humans have such tangly hair. Or that they do stupid things to it with spray and clips before a party. Or that they don't sort it out before going to bed." The squeaky one seemed annoyed.

Fine, now her inner voice was criticising her beauty routine. Just what she needed. She couldn't remember being tipsy, but then perhaps people never did. She remembered Douglas giving her a lift home, but he'd promised to do that anyway. She hoped she hadn't been sick in his car. He'd pointed out the mistletoe hanging in her porch, surely he wouldn't have mentioned it if she'd smelt of vomit? Mind you, his startled 'what's that up there?' was hardly the most romantic thing she'd ever heard.

Had she kissed him? How was it possible that she didn't know?

"Are you going to help me or what?" The shrill voices were back and the kicking had stopped, only to be replaced by a tugging sensation.

"Okay okay, I'm coming. Hold still or you'll just make it worse."

Emily couldn't tell which one of the two was asking for assistance. One was under her foot and the other was clinging to the back of her head. For once, she was glad the children were wrong about her having eyes there; the little person would now be treading on her lashes if she had.

She could feel her leg twitching. She supposed it was a

twitch though it felt as if a cat was climbing on her. Perhaps she had accidentally let in a cat last night? She opened her eyes to see. On top of her cream and blue quilt was a small, shiny, purple pixie.nHe waved. Emily relaxed, she understood what was happening. Obviously, she was still asleep and dreaming.

"I'm not small." Squeaky sounded petulant.

"You're not dreaming love," his companion told Emily.

"I'm not," Squeaky continued. "Well I am, but pixies are supposed to be small. I'm only three quarters of an inch shorter than average." Squeaky was beginning to squawk.

"You are small, even she noticed that and she doesn't even believe in us."

"She does in her dreams."

"But she's not dreaming."

"Yes she is," he insisted in a stage whisper, accompanied by a surprisingly large wink.

"Well it's gotta be large so she can see it through all that hair."

"Is he another Pixie?" Emily asked.

"No that's a leprechaun," said Squealy.

"Really?"

"No!"

Well how was she supposed to know? She couldn't see him.

"Because you're not on holiday in Ireland. Leprechauns is Irish. It's Christmas, so you get Pixies."

"I thought it was elves."

"Irish Elves?"

"No. Elves to help Santa."

"Do you see Santa?" asked Squeaky.

"No."

"Exactly. Elves just hang around him all day."

"Yes, Santa. No Santa. What a really excellent idea, Santa," they both chanted in an accent that, she guessed, was supposed to sound elf-like.

"If you want any work doing you need pixies."

"Is anyone going to help me out of this hair?"

Emily carefully sat up. The squealing pixie fell off her leg. She pushed the quilt gently aside, got out of bed and sat before the dressing table. She took the clips out of her hair and released the smaller pixie. Once they were stood side by side she could see that they were actually of a similar height.

"What work were you doing and how did you get in my hair?" she demanded.

"We was trying to sprinkle you and your drippy boyfriend with magic dust."

"Magic dust? Doesn't that belong to fairies?"

"You can't prove that," they both claimed.

"Why did you want to sprinkle it on me and Douglas, who is not the slightest bit interested in me, by the way?"

"He is too; poor lad got a double dose. Lanky here was supposed to do you but his berry broke and he feel, double-dosing dopey Douglas and landing in your hair."

"Is that why he's wearing that ridiculous hat?"

"What you on about now?" Squeaky was squawking again.

Too late, Emily realised they were wearing identical hats.

"You said something about damaging his beret."

"Pay attention will you. We have to get this sorted."

Emily tried to look patient.

"Well, what happened was, we heard how that rotten ex-husband of yours has been treating you."

"The divorce was mutual actually."

"Yeah, whatever," Squeaky agreed.

She wanted to argue but decided saving face in front of two imaginary pixies wasn't worth the effort. "Let's just sort things out so that I can go back to sleep."

The pixies explained that after her 'mutual parting' from her husband they had kept an eye on her. They felt responsible because the split had happened during the Christmas break and was on their patch.

"When you both found someone new we thought it would work out."

"Douglas is just a friend," Emily said.

"But could have been more."

Emily nodded. She had liked Douglas a lot and so had the children. Then Dave and his new wife had tried to get custody. She readily granted him access and would have agreed to joint custody. Dave however, was moving to America and wanted to take the children with him. Things had become unpleasant. Emily had stopped asking friends to baby-sit whilst she had the occasional evening out with Douglas. A visit to the pictures or a Chinese meal were not worth losing the children for. She'd pushed Douglas away completely.

"Time you and him got together. You need to get out more. You can't spend twenty-four hours a day with your children. It's not good for you or them."

Despite the squealing, and the fact that she was imagining all this, she knew he was making sense.

"So you decided to make us fall in love?"

"You already are, you just can't see it. He can but doesn't know what to do about it."

"What will happen to him?" asked Emily.

"Don't worry it wears off in a couple of days."

"Good. It would never have worked. It'll take more than stolen magic dust and a couple of pixies to sort my life out."

"Borrowed magic dust. And we've got more."

"What's the plan then?"

"Listen."

Emily listened and heard her children giggling.

"Goblins is teaching them a thing or too. Mrs Dave might go off the idea of taking them on full time. I suggest you let their dad spend all day tomorrow with them."

"Anything else?"

"Douglas will come round tomorrow. Make allowances, the dust is strong stuff and he's overdosed."

"All right. Can I go to sleep now?"

Emily awoke in the morning with a clear head and hazy memory of her odd dream. She got dressed quickly and made breakfast. She had a lot of Christmas shopping to do and a hundred and one other preparations to make for the whole holiday. The children were already over excited and she wasn't looking forward to dragging them round the shops.

The post arrived. Amongst the cards and circulars there was one very tiny envelope with festive decorations. It was addressed simply 'Emily'. There was nothing inside. The children said the envelope was so pretty she should hang it with the cards. As she held it up and clipped it into place some very fine, purple glitter fell onto her hair. The fairy lights fused.

The smoke alarm sounded; obviously the toast was ready. It almost drowned the ring of the telephone. Douglas quoted poetry at her then said he was coming round. She replaced the receiver just in time to stop the boys looking under the stairs where she had hidden some of their presents. They asked her if she had done kissing with Douglas yesterday.

She had an idea and picked up the phone again.

"Dave, look it's Christmas, let's try to be nice. You wanted to take the kids to a panto today. Okay you can. Come and collect them as soon as you like and you needn't bring them home 'til bedtime. Not too late though, we're driving up to Mum's tomorrow morning. We're staying with her for a couple of days."

Douglas arrived clutching an enormous bunch of flowers. She was trying to find vases whilst he was trying to declare undying love. Dave arrived and collected the children. His new wife waited in the car.

Douglas was obviously prepared to do anything she wanted. She felt a little guilty taking advantage of his kindness, but not guilty enough to refuse his help. He carried shopping, checked the car's tyre pressure, helped wrap presents then took her to lunch. She chose somewhere noisy so he couldn't whisper endearments. He fixed the fairy lights and then, as he already had the toolbox out, he mended the front gate which had been dragging for months. Whilst he was working, he stopped telling her that she was prettier than the angel on the tree. She found a lot of little jobs for him to do.

Douglas wanted to go dancing. Emily was surprised, she loved to dance, but he'd not been keen at last night's party. It was too good a chance to miss, but they didn't have long.

"I know a pub that has live music. We'd have a couple of hours if we left now."

Douglas wasn't a very good dancer but he tried hard. The slow dances were better. She liked being in his arms. On the way home she told him she was going away for a couple of days but would be back on Christmas Eve.

"The children are singing in a carol concert. Would you like to come?"

She knew that once she invited him into her life he'd want to stay there. This began to seem like a good thing.

David, his wife and the children arrived home at the same time as Emily.

"Emily can we talk? Please."

She handed Dave her key.

"Go and make some coffee."

She said good night to Douglas, who made good use of the mistletoe, then she went inside. The children were tired and for once went to bed when asked, without a fuss.

"Amanda and I have been thinking about what's best for the children." Dave held his wife's hand as he spoke. "Our arguments are just hurting them. You're doing a great job of caring for them."

"It can't always be easy," Amanda said, with feeling.

"We've spoken to them and they don't want to leave you or the country. We would like to see them regularly until we move in the spring. After that they should stay with you. Perhaps they could spend holidays with us. A few weeks in the summer and perhaps the half-terms. Could it work out?"

"Of course it could."

Dave and his wife left after arranging to meet at the carol concert.

"We'll bring the children's presents with us," Amanda said. "Will your friend be coming?"

"He certainly will. Hopefully that's another thing that's going to work out."

As Emily removed her make-up that night, she noticed she hadn't put away her hair clips. One of them felt sticky. There were mistletoe berries and purple glitter squashed onto it. How could that have happened?

15. Heavenly Bodies

The sun sank low, finally slipping below the horizon.

After him came the moon. As she rose, she looked down on their children. Beautiful combinations, of his bright warm light and her cool silent serenity, gazed back. They watched her from every pool and lake, each sea and ocean. Even tinkling streams carried a myriad of their tiny offspring.

She felt wistful that their father was so rarely able to fully see them. Tomorrow would be different; there was to be an eclipse.

He rose high into the clear blue. At once illuminating her and outshining her, so few realised she was beside him.

She inched ever closer.

For a moment he embraced her, smiling happily at the bright glimmers of smiles on their children's now darkened faces.

16. Portrait Of A Wife

Anne had been looking forward to having her portrait painted. Not because she was vain. Her face was attractive, but no more so than that of her sisters and they had greater youth as a further attraction. Neither was it entirely because of the things her family had said to her.

"This is an incredible chance for a girl like you," Mother had pointed out.

What she meant by a chance was the possibility that Anne might marry well. What she meant by a girl like her was one whose father had a modest title, excellent connections but little money. Naturally the title would not be passed to a daughter and Anne had no way to obtain a fortune other than by marriage, so those connections were all she had in her favour.

"Important, powerful people will see your image. If it's considered beautiful enough then they've promised it will be shown to Mr Holbein. If he likes what he sees there's a good chance he will come here and paint you for King Henry," Father had said.

His contacts had informed him that the influential court painter Hans Holbein was travelling to places such as France and Denmark to capture the likeness of potential brides. Their own modest home in Flanders would be no more difficult to reach. In order to persuade the famous artist the journey might be worthwhile, Father had hired another very talented painter. Although virtually unknown outside their town, it was rumoured that he could catch more than a likeness. Of course he would show her face and figure, and the sumptuous clothes and jewels Mother had borrowed for the occasion. If the rumours were true he would also capture the sweetness of her expression, the beauty of her thoughts, the nobility of her soul. Her parents were sure these things could win the love of a King.

It was because of the artist, Thomas, that Anne was looking forward to sitting for her portrait. She liked him a great deal. Although his manners were impeccable, his behaviour was subtly different from that of other men she'd met. He treated her as an equal. Not superior because of her pedigree, nor inferior because of her sex. Thomas considered that his own accomplishments and talents compensated for his relatively lowly birth. To him the fact that she was born female made her no less capable of holding interesting opinions, of learning about more than music, poetry, dancing and fine needlework.

Most surprising of all, he apparently persuaded Father of his point of view. One day he quoted Thomas, "If a man is to rise in the world, he must first understand how it works."

Anne, seeing her chance, pleaded the case for herself and was permitted to listen when her younger brothers' tutor instructed them in mathematics, philosophy and the way the stars circled the Earth. Thomas was welcomed to functions and in their home as warmly as any member of the nobility. Anne had hoped that, if she could persuade Thomas to ask, she would be permitted to marry him. That his suit would be as welcome as if he was a man of breeding and prestige who had gifts and power to bestow.

He did have gifts and power in a way. It would be a great honour for her family if King Henry of England chose Anne to be his bride and it would be exciting to be a queen. Thomas was their best hope of that. His talent was genuine. The match was Father's greatest wish. Anne understood it was something she should want, but she doubted it would happen. Henry was not only rich and powerful, but she'd heard he was wonderfully handsome, clever, chivalrous and a great sportsman. A man like that couldn't want her… could he?

At first the sitting was all she could want of it. Thomas flattered both Mother and Anne in a courtly manner and showed proper respect to Father and gratitude for being entrusted with the commission. He directed one of the maids to arrange Anne's clothes and posture so they were shown to best advantage whilst taking her comfort into consideration.

After a few sittings Anne noticed Mother seemed a little bored of chaperoning them.

"You have much to do, Mother. If you send Gertrude to me, I will be quite all right here," Anne offered.

So decorous was Thomas's manner that by the next sitting her parents decided it was safe to leave he and Anne with no one but that elderly maidservant to observe the proprieties.

Anne attempted first to flirt with Thomas and then when that failed, to converse intelligently on matters which she felt might interest him. When she gained his attention he seemed pleased she was growing more knowledgable and his behaviour was never dismissive, but she saw the greater part of his attention was concentrated on his task. Anne therefore amused herself with daydreaming about being the queen of England. She'd be adored not just by her husband but by their people. She would no longer be just a woman subjected to the will of men but someone important and powerful in her own right. The fantasy was pleasant.

The experience of Thomas studying her so closely was a reality and as such far more intoxicating. His eyes must be tracing the curve of her lips, the hollow of her throat and swell of her breasts. She felt herself blush at the thought and wondered if he'd paint her with that thought on her mind, or looking as demure and respectable as when Father was in the room.

Once Thomas realised that Gertrude was deaf, he said, "I wish I'd listened to my conscience and refused to take part in this terrible scheme."

"Do you not wish to paint my portrait, Thomas?"

"Not for this purpose."

"You do not wish to be the instrument of my advancement?"

"It would be your downfall, Anne. Do not mistake King Henry for the charming boy shown in ballads and masques. He has grown old, fat and cruel even to those he once loved or were his greatest allies."

"It cannot be true." Henry's virtues had been proclaimed for many years. Perhaps he was no longer a slender youth, rashly promoting and awarding anyone who flattered or pleased him, but he would not have changed so very much. Now he would be mature, dignified. Kind and gentle.

"Your marriage to Henry would not bring happiness to … to those who care for you."

Of course it would. Father would be delighted and the prospects of her sisters greatly improved. Why was Thomas saying such things? In truth she didn't want to be taken across the sea, away from all she knew to live amongst strangers in a foreign land. She didn't want her only opportunity to see Thomas to involve pleading with the king that an artist from her former home be brought to paint the princes it would be her duty to produce. If Henry was really the man she'd grown up to believe he was, whom she'd worked hard to convince herself she should care for, then she trusted she could be content with her fate. It was not her first choice though, had not been for some time.

"Don't marry him, Anne, I beg of you."

That was more like it. A woman had to marry, so he must have another suitor in mind. Himself?

"What choice do I have?" she asked, half smiling at him in invitation. That was his cue to declare his love. Surely Father would agree, would place her happiness over his own ambitions?

"You have none," Thomas said. "A woman must do as she's bid."

Anne knew he was right, but didn't like to hear him say it. She was just a pawn to be used by others in an attempt to raise themselves higher. Just as Father wished to profit from her hoped-for marriage, Thomas also stood to gain. As the artist who found a wife for King Henry his future would be assured. It was in his interests to paint her as well as he was able.

As Thomas worked, she tried to take pleasure in his attention. Sometimes it worked. When she saw his brush loaded with paint in the same pale cream as her skin or rich chestnut of her hair, she imagined him gently stroking and caressing her. But when he switched to the glowing colours of the jewels she was bedecked with, it seemed he too was selling her to the highest bidder. Only the wish to have this torment over as quickly as possible allowed her to sit still.

The painting, when finally it was finished, was a shock to

Anne. The background against which she was depicted was no longer the finest room in her father's modest home, but somewhere far grander. More splendid surely than anywhere King Henry had ever called home. Anne's dress was no longer fashioned from good silk, instead it seemed to have been woven from precious metals interwoven with the finest strands of gossamer. No mortal hand could have stitched anything so intricate, so regal. The borrowed jewels didn't sparkle; they glowed with fire, like raindrops in the sun scattering a rainbow of colour.

Anne's hair gleamed, her eyes shone, her skin was radiant. Her pose and figure were modest yet noble. Everything was just as it should be and yet ... There was something. Although she looked like a young woman who would submit to marrying a stranger, could accept a new life in another country and rise to the challenge of being queen, there was no sign of her wishing to do so.

Thomas must have done that on purpose, perhaps thinking modesty, even a hint of reluctance, might seem attractive to Henry. There had been rumours that Anne Boleyn had lacked such qualities and that had displeased Henry. But then there were so many rumours.

Father was delighted with the portrait. He paid Thomas handsomely and told all who would listen of his talent. Many did listen and they too commissioned portraits from him. His fame and finances rose quickly. His place in society rose too as he became accepted into the homes of ever more powerful men. It was said he painted their wives' and daughters' likenesses to be hung in great halls and sketched other women to decorate smaller, darker rooms.

As her family waited for news of how Anne's portrait was received, more creditable rumours were heard of the reasons

King Henry was in need of a new wife. Such things weren't knowingly said in front of Anne of course, but she sometimes contrived to be close enough to hear.

"Sources I trust claim he put aside his first wife not for the will of God, but to fulfil his own desires," Father said to Thomas. "Could such a thing be true?"

"I very much fear that this and still worse is true. I hear that his second wife died because she could not bear him a son and the third because she did. It's even said he's refused to accept the authority of the holy Roman emperor."

"No man could do such a thing, not even a king," Anne declared, forgetting she was pretending to be too far away to hear.

"Henry is like no other man," Thomas declared.

Father, she noted looked troubled. "I wish now that I'd never hired you, Thomas or that your talent were not so great. Have greed and ambition blinded me to the truth?" he asked. "Did I see not my beloved daughter, but a step upward?"

Anne knew the answer to that could be nothing but yes. He hadn't stopped loving her and some of the ambition he'd felt had been for her, but surely he'd made a terrible choice.

"You asked me to portray Anne to best advantage," Thomas said. "You requested I show more than just the surface, that I let her true self shine through in order that her future be assured."

"I know, I know. Don't think I blame you."

"You misunderstand me. You did what you thought best at the time, as did I. It is my greatest hope that my talent is all that it's claimed to be and that Hans Holbein too is as great as his reputation and recognises the qualities I've committed to canvas."

"I don't understand," Father said, echoing Anne's own thoughts.

Thomas opened the sketch book he habitually carried.

"As I painted Anne we sometimes talked together, of our lives here, of things we enjoy or admire, dare I say even of our friendship."

"Did you indeed?" Father spoke abruptly, but not with the anger such a statement would once have provoked.

Thomas quickly continued. "At other times I was absorbed in my work and Anne was left with her own thoughts. Those I believe were of the reason for the portrait, of what her life would be if she were indeed selected as the bride of King Henry. Am I correct, Anne?"

She agreed that he was and stepped closer, hoping for a glimpse of the drawings.

"This one shows her expression as I painted it for Mr Holbein and the king. And this shows … "

A messenger arrived, his entrance preventing Anne from hearing his final words.

"My lord, the King of England has chosen a new wife."

"Already?"

"The news came here first, because the new queen is from this very place."

"Not Anne, tell me it's not Anne!"

"But it is, my lord. Anne of Cleves. The lady sails to him now."

Anne heard her own sigh of relief echoed by the two men she loved the most. The messenger was rewarded with coin and sent to the kitchen for meat and wine.

"Thomas, you too must be rewarded," Father said.

"There is just one thing I desire."

For a moment it seemed Father was as puzzled as Anne, but then he looked again at the sketch book and nodded. "I've made one mistake in that direction already. I'll not make another. Daughter, when you are asked, you have my leave to respond as you wish."

Anne wanted to ask what he meant, but Father handed her the book and as she looked at the drawings he walked away. Both sketches were her… but they were so different. One face she recognised as that which Thomas had painted into her portrait for Henry. It wasn't unkind or unflattering or untrue, but Anne could see why the image would not have appealed to the King. It showed too plainly that she did not wish to be his queen.

"I believe that's how I looked when I imagined leaving my home, my family, friends." One friend most of all, but it wasn't proper for her to say so.

The other sketch made her blush, in imitation of the flush he'd shaded onto her cheeks. She tried hard not to recall her thoughts of him caressing her skin with his brush, stroking her lips on the page.

"This one … you painted me like this?"

"Yes, but only for one man. I hope he's the only man you'll ever look at that way. Your husband."

"No! What Father said … he meant, I'm sure he meant, that it would be my choice whom I marry."

"As indeed it shall. So Anne, will your true portrait remain forever hidden away, or shall I frame it and hang it on my wall?"

17. Copycat

Two days ago, I had my hair cut. I like to be different and my hairstyles often reflect that. This time I've really made a statement. It's an asymmetric cut; very short above my left ear, spiralling around my shoulders down almost to my waist as it falls over my right shoulder. It's vibrant red, except for blonde tips to my straight fringe. The look is dramatic and I'd thought it was original. Then I got a call from my hairdresser.

"I'm really sorry, Chloe, but Melissa offered me an extra £100 to recreate your style."

I couldn't be angry with the stylist. Her husband was made redundant on the very day she'd discovered she was pregnant. She needs the money, and Melissa who has more than enough of the stuff, obviously realised that.

"If you want to change yours, I'll redo it for nothing. I really am sorry, Chloe."

"I'll think about it, but don't worry; it's not your fault. Melissa always gets what she wants."

It's true, Melissa has always got whatever she's wanted. This wouldn't be so bad except for one thing; what she wants is whatever I happen to have. It's not just my hairstyle, there's Tim too. I've been seeing less of him because he's been seeing more of her. A lot more, if you catch my drift.

I'd realised what she was like within a few days of her

joining my school a dozen years ago. She'd been the new girl; I'd been the popular one. My friends and popularity had been what she'd wanted then. She'd set out to win them, by befriending me. I'd been easy to win over. Her rich parents took us skiing, to pop concerts and theme parks. Melissa always had the latest clothes and music CDs and she lent them to me. She got enough pocket money for sweets, magazines and lipsticks for herself and anyone she liked. I was invited on the family holiday to Corfu. She easily persuaded me to call her my friend.

Once she became an accepted part of my group, she wanted to be the one to decide what we'd do and where we'd go. As she, or rather her parents, paid for nearly everything, she had no trouble persuading the rest of us to go along with her plans. It didn't take long before our circle of friends started changing. The shallow, fashionable crowd hung around with us. The more interesting girls, the ones with enough personality to have their own ideas, drifted away.

By the time I realised I didn't like Melissa much, it was too late. My old friends weren't interested any more after I'd neglected them in favour of things Melissa could buy.

All Melissa's ideas were mine. If I suggested something, she'd come up with a bigger, pricier version of the same thing. Imitation is supposed to be flattering, but it just annoyed me. I felt like the own-label offer in comparison to her brand-leader image. I didn't want to be like her. She didn't want to be like me either; I think she actually wanted to be me.

I'd imagined that after leaving school I wouldn't see much of Melissa. I wanted to become a beautician and went to college to train. Of course, Melissa also declared she'd be a beautician, although she had no intention of struggling through college. She got her father to buy a share in a beauty parlour and ensure she was given a job there.

Melissa often rang, inviting me for drinks or meals out. As a hard-up student I was an easy target, rarely finding the strength to refuse. Once I qualified as a beautician and was earning some money, I moved out of Mum's place and into a bed-sit. Melissa's father bought her a two bedroom apartment in the same block.

Tim lived on the same floor as me. He shared a flat with his friend, Duncan. Tim helped carry up all my stuff when I moved in. I'd cooked a meal to thank him and we'd soon become friends. I'd spend as many evenings in Tim's flat as in my own. We'd watch videos and often I'd cook for Tim and Duncan.

When Melissa moved in, her Daddy hired a removal firm, so she didn't need any help. I invited her round for a drink, just to be polite. I hoped she'd changed. She brought champagne and ordered in Chinese food. She asked all sorts of questions about my life, rather than just talking about herself. She did seem to have grown up a bit. After a couple of glasses of champagne, I told her about Tim, what a nice man he is and how much I liked him.

When she met Tim, Melissa again saw something she thought would be better as hers than mine. She immediately went all out to get him.

Whenever I was at Tim's, she would pop in, apparently looking for me. I worked Friday evenings; coincidentally Melissa would often get hold of concert tickets for Fridays.

"Oh, Chloe, what a shame you can't come. It would have been so much fun."

"I'm sure you'll still enjoy it, Melissa," Tim would say. She always managed to ensure he was within earshot of these conversations.

"I wouldn't want to go on my own; I don't suppose you'd like to come?"

Tim was naturally flattered by all her attention, not to mention the gifts she bought him. Quite often, when I went to Tim's flat he wasn't in. Duncan told me who he was with.

I look in the mirror at my lovely new hairstyle. I won't change it. Red suits me better than it does Melissa. She didn't start growing her hair long until she'd realised that's what I was doing, so the unusual style will be less effective on her. Also, as I'd agreed to be photographed for an advertisement for the salon, everyone will know my cut is the original. Melissa and her hair are just a second-rate copy of me.

It's time I had a little chat with Melissa.

"Chloe, we need to talk," she says before I can get a word in.

"Funny, I was just about to say the same thing."

"There's something I have to tell you."

"Go on."

It's about Tim. I feel bad, you've always been my friend and we've shared so much, but there are some things we can't share."

"Like Tim?" I ask.

"Yes. I know you like him, but so do I. A girl's got to go after what she wants."

"Well you do, anyway." I look at her hair. It isn't identical to mine; it's shaped in a mirror image, only less dramatic. The tips are black, not blonde. It looks good though, almost as good as mine. "Melissa, what exactly is it you've come to say?"

"I've asked Tim to move in with me. He's agreed."

"Well, of course he has."

"You're not angry?"

"Oh, didn't I tell you? Perhaps I should have as we're such dear friends. Duncan and I are engaged." I hold up my hand to show her the ring I'd forgotten to tell her about. "I'll be moving in with him just as soon as Tim moves out."

18. Dear Andy

'Dear Andy,' she writes.

Can she do that; use an endearment to start the letter telling her husband she's leaving?

'Andy.'

Too hard. He is a dear man, just not the man Linda wants.

'I want to tell you', but she doesn't want to. She wants Justin, but not to hurt anyone. Linda's hurting. What will Andy do without her?

Tears splash on the page. Linda crumples the letter and starts over.

'Dear Andy,

I'm sorry to say ...'

She won't dump him by letter of course. That's not fair. She'll tell him face to face, but it'll be easier if she's thought it out first. Not easy, just easier. If she can't say the words she'll give him the letter, be there when he reads it, then gone forever.

'Dear Andy,

I'm very sorry to tell you ...'

Why's this so hard? She's made her decision. She wants Justin. To kiss him, hold him, sleep with him, wake with him. She wants to gaze into his big, brown eyes. Lashes long and dark as any romantic hero, though the irises aren't quite the traditional pools of liquid chocolate. More a rich caramel like the sauce she makes for special desserts. Desserts for dinners with Andy.

Stop it, Linda. Concentrate. Justin. Justin's strong arms holding her tight. Justin's hot breath against her neck, soft lips brushing her cheek in greeting. Hands that linger temptingly before he drags them away. And the time he didn't. Andy was away working. Justin came round, said he'd forgotten she was alone. He brought wine, her favourite. They drank. Kissed. They didn't do much more than that, not really. It wasn't as though they'd actually… She didn't tell Andy. Lied in fact. Kept on lying.

Justin visited her at work a few days later. It was raining, he offered her a lift. It gave her a lift just to get close for the polite kiss with which she always greeted her husband's friend. That wasn't what Justin meant. He meant more and she wanted more. She'd got wet dashing across the car park, holding his hand and laughing. Hot, wet, frustrated; she had to go home to her husband.

Justin sent texts. Jokes mostly. Nothing wrong in sharing a joke with a friend. Sometimes they'd chat. She mentioned she could finish work early. So could he, how about a coffee or something? They'd opted for something. It wasn't much. Not an affair, not that. It was just … exciting. Everything about Justin is exciting. The way he looks at her, whispers her name, kisses her, touches. Justin always smells good, his skin's always smooth. He's never reluctant to talk, more interested in the TV or just plain grumpy.

Has Andy noticed? She never rushes home early to greet him in a loose dress, with hair slightly damp from the shower and something good bubbling on the stove. She used to when they were first married. The food almost ready but not eaten until hours later. Then she'd be in a loose nightie, her hair again damp from the shower. That was a long time ago. Things change.

Linda's changed. When she lies in bed on Sunday mornings she isn't listening to Andy's steady breathing hoping to hear the change that means he's waking. She doesn't long for him to reach out for her. Linda lies in bed with Andy, thinking of Justin. Lying. She doesn't shave her legs on Friday ready for weekends with her husband; she wants them smooth for weekdays when she might see Justin. And she feels guilty.

Andy hasn't changed. He looks a little older, but they all do. He's just as kind, but she's used to that. He's just as clever and funny, but his jokes aren't new. Her husband still loves her and wants her and makes love to her. She's used to it. She enjoys it still, but it's not fresh and exciting. It's sensible, married love. It doesn't make her feel young and wild and guilty.

Has Justin changed? Hard to tell. She'd not noticed him much before the Christmas party. She'd squeezed into a dress she hadn't been able to fasten the year before, nor the one before that. Andy hadn't said a word about how she looked. Justin had. He'd said it in words and with his eyes and with his thigh pressed against hers when they sat to eat.

Perhaps he's always been the sort to seduce the wife of a friend. Maybe she isn't the first woman he's pulled into his arms, whispered, 'we can't do this' and bent his head to kiss slowly and gently until she whimpers with longing. He hadn't tried it before she lost weight. Hadn't been there holding her hand and stroking away tears when she'd learned there'd be no children. Hadn't sworn she was everything to him when she'd felt she was nothing at all.

What was she doing? Andy is her husband. Her love. Justin is a few kisses. Exciting, very exciting, but that's not love.

Another sheet of paper. Another opening that isn't right.

'Dear Justin,

I'm sorry ...'

This letter she'll have to post. She can't give it to him without brushing his hand and wanting his touch everywhere. She can't hear him speak her name without watching his lips and wanting them on hers. She can write the letter though. She will post it. Will end this.

19. Something For The Weekend?

Gemma loved her Saturday job at the pharmacy. It wasn't as glamorous as the clothes store and didn't seem such a good place to meet boys as the music megastore but it was close to home and her boss, Mr Cantrell, was kind.

She soon realised it wasn't just sick people who used a pharmacy. Her first customer was an attractive young man who bought a toothbrush. She rang in the price, counted back his change and put his purchase in a paper bag, just as Mr Cantrell taught her.

By lunchtime, Gemma had served a variety of customers. Retired people more interested in chatting than buying, or harassed mothers looking for quick answers and quicker service. There had also been two more young men, both of whom bought toothbrushes.

As she ate her sandwiches, Gemma said, "I think I'm getting used to the till, now, Mr Cantrell."

"Yes, dear, you're doing very well. I can see you're going to be a great help, not to mention increasing sales of toothbrushes."

Before Gemma could ask what he meant, another customer arrived. It was 'fabulous' Phil, from the school football team. Although Gemma had watched every game, she'd never spoken to him. When he'd finished High School last summer, she thought she'd lost her chance.

"I'll serve this one, Mr Cantrell. You finish your lunch."

"Thank you."

As she returned to the shop floor and Phil looked up and gave her a beaming smile, she thought perhaps it was she who should be thanking her boss.

Phil actually spoke to her.

"Hi Gemma, I didn't know you worked here."

He knew her name!

"I started last week, how can I help?"

He selected a toothbrush.

"Just this, thanks."

He gave her a lovely smile, allowing her to appreciate his clean, white teeth.

"See you," he said as he left.

Gemma really loved her job.

The next week, Gemma sold several more toothbrushes, including another one to Phil. He did have lovely teeth, but it seemed odd he'd want another one so soon. She remembered Mr Cantrell saying she'd increase the sale of toothbrushes and asked what he'd meant.

"Well, you see we sell all kinds of items here, sometimes customers are a little embarrassed about their requirements."

Gemma nodded, she had noticed young women seemed to prefer her to serve them when they bought personal items.

Mr Cantrell said, "Some of the lads might really want toothbrushes of course, but that's not what they usually buy when I serve them."

"Oh, you mean …" Gemma blushed. "Perhaps you should give me a sign when it might be better for you to serve?"

When Phil came in again, Mr Cantrell didn't make the agreed sign, so Gemma served him. Phil bought another toothbrush. He seemed nervous as he chatted to her.

"You've got nice eyes," he said.

She nearly told him how great his smile was, but stopped in time as she remembered what Mr Cantrell had said about toothbrushes. Phil couldn't really need a new one every week.

"Does he ever buy anything other than toothbrushes?" she asked her boss, after she'd served Phil.

"Oh yes, dear."

Phil was flirting with her despite apparently already having a girlfriend. What sort of girl did he think she was? The following week Phil selected two toothbrushes and baby oil.

"Planning an exciting weekend?" she asked.

"These are for next weekend, but yes, I'm expecting a good time. Perhaps you'd like to join me?"

What a cheek!

"Gemma, could you just give me a hand here?" Mr Cantrell called, before she could say anything.

He pointed to a box he was unpacking then served Phil.

"I think I should explain something, Gemma. That young man has taken a liking to you. I think you feel the same way?"

Gemma nodded.

"I didn't guess he'd ask so soon, or I'd have said something sooner."

"Shy? But the toothbrushes, and you said he bought other things…"

Mr Cantrell laughed. "He really does want the brushes and the other things he buys are cotton buds. I'll let him explain."

Gemma hadn't realised Phil was still in the shop.

"I've got an old car I've been doing up. The toothbrushes help me polish the grill and other fiddly bits of metalwork. I'm taking part in a vintage car rally next Saturday afternoon, would you like to come?"

She looked at Mr Cantrell.

"I'll let you finish early, if you like," he said.

Phil arrived to collect her in a gleaming open topped car. He opened the door for her, like a proper gentleman.

"I'll just be a moment," he said and went into the pharmacy.

Gemma tried not to speculate about what he could be buying. She didn't want to misjudge him again.

He handed her a huge pair of sunglasses.

"I don't want you getting anything blown into your pretty eyes," he said, before driving her away.

20. Looking After Trevor

I'd ordered coffee and a cake for Juliet, even though I knew she wouldn't want to eat after I'd said my piece.

"I'm sorry to tell you this, but I've heard rumours Trevor's been flirting with one of the barmaids down the Pint and Pencil. To be honest, I'm not surprised. Lately all you do is moan about him and you've let yourself go a bit."

She'd been struggling to chew and swallow as I'd been speaking. Eventually she managed it. "Reckon he's been doing a lot more than flirting! He's out all hours and comes home smelling of perfume and twice he's had lipstick on him."

"That's what I mean! You act like you don't trust him and complain when he's working late to put a roof over your head."

She started to cry, which made me feel bad, but really she had to be told. I did what I could to cheer her up then suggested she go home, have a long hot bath and make something nice for Trevor's dinner.

"Good idea, Freya, thanks. He said he'd be late again so I've got time to do something special."

"Must go, I've got a date. Have to tidy myself up."

"You look wonderful as you are!" Juliet said.

I smiled. I tried to look nice all the time but made an extra effort when my man was due. Didn't want him looking elsewhere, did I?

As soon as Juliet left, I rang Trevor. "The coast is clear for this evening. Juliet's going to be busy and she thinks you're working late."

"OK, Pussycat," he whispered huskily. "Wear that frilly little pink number for me."

I didn't feel guilty that night. It was lovely to have him to myself all evening. Usually we made do with a snatched half hour on his way home from work, or when he popped round to put up a shelf. That man was good with his hands in more ways than one!

Nor did I feel guilty during the following weeks as Juliet looked more and more haggard, moaned Trevor paid her little attention and was irritable with everyone. If she didn't appreciate him, rarely bothered with make-up and never smiled, was it any wonder he was forced to seek comfort elsewhere?

I did feel guilty when she called to say she had to go into hospital. "I have a favour to ask, Freya."

"Of course, anything."

"It's Trevor. Poor man. I've been in pain and so worried about the operation I've neglected him and let myself go, just like you said. He works so hard I can't expect him to nurse me when I come out so I was thinking of going to my sister's for a few weeks."

"Good idea, but what is it you want me to do?" I asked.

"Take care of him while I'm away. Give him dinner once in a while, fetch a bit of shopping, see he's not lonely, that sort of thing."

"I'd be happy to! Don't you worry, I'll take really good care of him."

"Yes, I imagine you will."

I didn't like the way she said that, but quickly dismissed it. This was my chance to show Trevor how much better off he'd be with me.

As soon as Trevor dropped Juliet at the hospital he came round to me. We had a lovely day together, walking and laughing in the autumn sunshine until the sky darkened and the air cooled.

"Nearly dinnertime," he said.

"Yes, I'm hungry." I'd not known how long he'd be at the hospital so hadn't eaten lunch. "Where shall we go?"

"I've been looking forward to your marvellous cooking. Juliet's done no more than open tins lately."

"OK, right." I smiled brightly as I tried to think of something that wouldn't require hours of preparation. "I'll have to go to the shop for a few things," I said.

He drove us straight back to my place, went to the fridge and poured himself a glass of the good wine I'd been saving for a special occasion. Of course it was a special occasion in a way.

"You'd better not have any if you're going down the shop," he said.

Luckily the nearest shop stocks a good range of fresh ingredients, albeit at a premium price. I tried not to wince as the storekeeper rang up the smoked salmon, king prawns, cream, and strawberries.

It didn't take me long to whip up a pretty little starter with the salmon, hull the strawberries, put tagliatelle on to boil and create a delicate creamy sauce. Not long enough in fact, as the film Trevor was watching hadn't finished. Instead of sitting at the beautifully laid table and gazing at each other in the candlelight, he asked me to bring in the food on a tray.

By the time I'd finished the washing up, Trevor was asleep in my bed. I hadn't realised he snored quite so loudly. Juliet had moaned about that and the fact he refused to wear the nose clip that would have allowed her a peaceful night's sleep. With regret I remembered pointing out the clip might be tight or painful and that she should be used to his snoring by now.

I must have got to sleep eventually as Trevor woke me to ask for toast. "You won't have time to cook anything else and iron my shirt."

When he'd gone I spent an hour getting shaving foam off the sink and mopping up the result of a mini tsunami in the bathroom. I shopped and cooked so his dinner would be ready the minute he got in and before he could settle in front of the television. It was overdone by the time he got back from the hospital. Tactfully I didn't mention that he'd said he was just going to pop in for half an hour and instead suggested that next time he ring and let me know when he'd be back.

"Oh dear, another jealous woman!" he'd said in what I hoped was a jokey tone.

That weekend I saw Trevor for less time than we'd previously managed during a whole week when Juliet was home. By the time he'd played golf, had 'a swift half' with his mates and visited his wife, there wasn't time for me.

On Monday he came in earlier than I'd expected.

"Juliet's sister was with her, so I didn't need to stay." He looked at my unmade up face, disarranged hair and flour covered clothes as though to say he now regretted that. He watched TV whilst I finished dinner preparations and was snoring before I'd finished the washing up.

I visited Juliet in hospital the following day. She was sat in a chair laughing over something in a magazine. She looked well rested and had applied a slick of lipstick. Her eyes shone, her hair was glossy. Although I'd fallen asleep after clearing up the breakfast things it hadn't helped that much as I'd woken up stiff in my chair and had no time for make-up if I was to make visiting hours.

"Thank you so much, Freya," she said as I sank down onto the edge of her bed. "Trevor has told me how well you're looking after him."

"Huh! More than he's done to me. Not exactly over generous with appreciation and compliments, is he?"

"That's not his style. I suppose he thinks if he's paying for the food then he's done his bit," Juliet said.

"Hmmm." He'd given me money for 'housekeeping' but it wasn't enough for fine wines, seafood and fresh strawberries even once a week and he expected good food every night. Maybe Juliet hadn't been exaggerating as much as I'd thought when she said she didn't have enough money left to buy scent and pretty lingerie. I'd not believed it because he'd been generous with gifts for me. Had, past tense. It was quite a while since he'd brought me any prettily wrapped packages.

I was delighted to learn Juliet was leaving hospital the next day. My happiness faded as she reminded me she was going to her sister's. When she said she'd be there a month, I panicked.

"Juliet, you can't! Remember what you said about him having an affair?" She tried to interrupt but I wouldn't let her. "He might not be there when you come back."

"Oh, I think he will. Absence makes the heart grow fonder, so they say. Of course I won't be able to cook for ages, or do the shopping or ironing so he's going to have to do all that. It won't leave much time for his lady friend. Still enough of me and my troubles, how are you, my friend?"

"Fed up," I admitted.

"Well you don't want to spend all your time moaning; men don't like that. You might want to consider your appearance too. You've let yourself go a bit lately. If you don't make a bit more of an effort then Trevor, oh sorry, I mean your mystery man, is going to look elsewhere."

21. Never Say Never

One of my earliest memories of my Godmother, whom I called Aunt Phoebe, is of us passing a bus stop where a couple were kissing.

"Euw, I'm never doing that. It's gross!"

She'd just laughed and said, "Never say never, Jenny."

I told her I'd never like school. All those people telling me what I could and couldn't do, yet none were properly interested in me like Aunt Phoebe was. She taught me how to dunk cookies without the end dropping off. Or how to tame a robin so he'd take food right from my hand, or how to make a hula hoop go round and round for hours without crashing to the ground. Why couldn't I go to her house every day instead of boring old school?

"I'll never understand fractions," I wailed when I stayed in her terraced house the week my baby brother was born.

And then, "He cries all the time and smells, I'll never like him," during my next visit.

"Never say never," she said before offering to help with my maths homework. She placed a freshly baked cake on the table. "If you can divide this into eighths, you can eat one of them."

With an incentive like that I soon grasped that her eighth and mine added up to one quarter and three quarters of the cake remained, meaning six more slices for us to enjoy. She was right about my brother too. He soon became an adorable toddler who I loved to push on the swings and play hide and seek with.

"I'll never get the point of poetry," I told her once and another day, "No way will I give Jonathan Pemberton my phone number."

Aunt Phoebe laughed at both of those, told me never to say never and asked what the poor boy had done.

"He's a geek and sooo boring. We have zero in common."

Of course I was a kid back then. Thankfully I grew up. For a start I began to realise I wasn't the centre of the known universe. I saw my little brother struggling with maths at school and helped him understand fractions by breaking his chocolate bar into pieces. As there were nine squares I had to eat one to make things easier, but that was a sacrifice I was willing to make for the sake of his education.

When Aunt Phoebe suggested we visit museums and galleries as a change from funfairs or shopping trips I agreed and surprised myself by enjoying the visits, even if that was mainly because of the tea shops.

I kissed boys too, not Jonathan Pemberton obviously, but quite a few others. My exam results were terrible.

"I'll never get a decent job," I told Aunt Phoebe, repeating what my teachers had been saying all through the previous year.

I was hoping for her usual reassuring words, but she said, "Not unless you put in a bit of effort."

"It wasn't my fault." I made the same excuses that I'd been making to myself; my brother's music was too distracting, I couldn't tell boyfriends I'd prefer to stay in revising than go out with them, there were too many other, more important things to do. Even as I said it all, the word 'never' echoed in my head and I knew I wasn't being honest. My brother would have used headphones if I'd asked. I didn't truly need a date every night. Important though it was to get my hair and make-up perfect, maybe getting some qualifications should also feature on my list of priorities.

Aunt Phoebe suggested I stay on another year and retake my exams. I could come to her house and study.

"Won't that be boring for you?" I asked.

"I'll work too," she said.

We started when I arrived straight from school each afternoon and continued until we heard, through the partition wall, her neighbour's TV reporting the news headlines at seven.

Poetry, that's what she worked at. She was a freelance writer, but I'd never realised that while factual articles earned her money, poetry was her passion. She'd won a few awards and had dozens of them published. I should have known about that, shouldn't I? Should have shut up about myself long enough for her to tell me.

Realising that and remembering my, 'I'll never get poetry' comment I apologised.

"It doesn't matter, Jenny. You don't need to be the same as someone to love them."

"Don't write one about me," I said one evening when I realised her pen had stopped and she was watching me intently.

"Never!" she said.

I didn't need to look up again to see the laughter on her face.

Although I had to become almost as boring as Jonathan Pemberton to do it, I got good grades. So good in fact that I enrolled for further education.

When I got my first job, Aunt Phoebe said, "That's wonderful. I never doubted you."

"What never?" I teased.

"Well, almost never. Certainly not as much as I doubted myself, but I've had good news too. We should go out to celebrate."

After we'd ordered champagne and our meal, Aunt Phoebe gave me a book of poems. Her poems. The title read, 'Never Say Never' and inside the formal dedication; 'To Jenny, my inspiration always.' She'd written the title in hand under that and signed it for me. Good thing our wine came then or I'd have embarrassed us both by crying.

The poems were beautiful, wonderful. Gorgeous glimpses into our shared memories. She didn't name me other than in the dedication, but when she described the child with a dab of chocolate frosting on her nose I knew the kid had my freckles and appetite. She didn't name the galleries we'd walked round together, nor the beaches we'd combed for shells, but I saw them again as I read her verses. Each line was as reassuring as her laughing rebuttal whenever I'd declared myself unable to do something.

Aunt Phoebe's neighbour told her he was moving into a home.

"I don't want to do that," Aunt Phoebe said. She didn't say she never would though and neither did I, though I promised myself I'd do what I could to help her manage where she was.

Jonathan Pemberton moved in next door. That's not as much of a coincidence as it sounds. Ours is a very small town with very few houses within the price range of a single person. Jonathan was a good neighbour. He waved to Aunt Phoebe each morning as he went to work and gave her a lift to the supermarket when he went himself. He opened jars and changed light bulbs. Naturally we met from time to time. He must have remembered the sneering way I'd refused his attempts to ask me out, but he never made me feel bad about it. I did feel bad though.

I didn't give him my phone number; Aunt Phoebe did that with my full consent and passed on his. It made sense for him to be able to reach me if he was ever concerned about her. She gave him a front door key too. Just as well.

Aunt Phoebe had a dizzy spell and stumbled down the stairs. Jonathan heard and went round to see if she was OK. He had to let himself in as she was too dazed to do it. He called for an ambulance and called me. She was badly bruised and shocked, but there was no long-term damage. The dizziness was due to an ear infection which quickly responded to antibiotics and she was back home again, baking her wonderful cakes in less than a week.

It could have been so much worse. Had Jonathan not heard, or not gone to investigate, she'd have lain there all night. The heating wasn't on and she was just wearing her nightie.

"I'll never be able to thank you," I told him.

"Oh, never say never," he said and winked.

I knew where he'd got that expression from! He'd not have got to hear it though if Aunt Phoebe hadn't liked him enough to have proper conversations with him, the kind where you talk about your fears and your hopes. They probably didn't have much in common, but they certainly liked each other. As she'd said, you don't need to be the same to care.

"I could try by taking you out to dinner, if you'd like?" I said.

"I would like that," Jonathan said.

I think maybe we might become friends. I doubt it'll ever be more than that, but as Aunt Phoebe says, never say never. After all, I'd once said I hated school, didn't see the point of poetry and would never understand fractions. Now I'm a primary school teacher and encourage my class to create their own verses and calculate fractions using a pack of cookies. It's not impossible that those children will one day stop calling me Miss Jones and start addressing me as Mrs Pemberton.

22. From Wine Gums To Candy Canes

Elly stood outside the fancy hotel and looked up at Dover Castle illuminated high above her. As teenagers she and her husband Mark had often gone there. Not actually inside, as they couldn't afford that, but they'd cycled as close as they could and picnicked somewhere with a good view. Despite the National Trust rules, they'd camped on the nearby white cliffs some weekends. They'd made their plans, dreamed their dreams and toasted it all in wine gums. They used to make do with what they had, make the most of any chance to enjoy themselves. These days she got in a tizzy if the supermarket were out of parma ham and had to make do with prosciutto instead. Although the castle entrance fee could now be easily afforded, they'd not made the time to visit. So many other, less fun things, seemed more important.

Her thoughts were interrupted by a group of people coming out to smoke. Elly shivered. It was cold and lonely out on the street, but no more so than back in that over-heated hotel. Or back in their tastefully appointed, centrally heated house which took the place of a cosy, joy filled home. She'd never before felt cold and lonely in Dover. It was where Mark first told her he loved her. It was where, twelve years ago he'd proposed. Twelve years exactly.

They'd stayed in a Bed and Breakfast then, drunk real wine to celebrate. They'd been so happy, but looking forward to an even better future. Was that when they'd taken their first step in the wrong direction?

Half an hour earlier, Elly had been standing next to her husband, surrounded by people, and feeling completely alone. Although she recognised some of the people 'mingling' in the fancy hotel, there wasn't anyone she knew. Well, there was Mark of course. She knew her own husband, didn't she? Sometimes she wondered if she even knew herself. She definitely didn't know why they were there.

She was aware they'd driven down to Dover, stopped outside the hotel and handed their car keys to the concierge as they checked in. She knew they'd changed into evening wear and walked down to the ballroom. Elly clearly remembered the imposingly dressed man who'd opened the door for them with great ceremony.

"Good evening, madam, sir. Do enjoy your evening."

They'd not been announced, Mark's rank within the company wasn't sufficiently elevated for that. Not yet anyway. They'd been offered champagne though and presented with trays of pretty canapés.

Her understanding was perfectly clear on some other points too. Mark had told her that, partly for reasons of political correctness, the company he worked for would be holding a New Year's Eve party rather than the traditional Christmas version.

The ritual of attempting to buy a dress which was mainstream enough for her not to seem odd or unfashionable, yet unusual enough that no other guest would arrive wearing the same thing, had been observed. Just the once that year thankfully. She'd already worn it to her own work event, knowing there would be time to get it dry cleaned had that proved necessary.

Elly and Mark hadn't been sat together for the dinner. "The directors prefer people to mingle," Mark explained.

Elly, and she suspected most other guests of employees, spent the meal in dull small talk with people she didn't know and most likely would never meet again. Things didn't get a whole lot more fun after she was reunited with Mark. Conversation was so safe and polite that hundreds of words were used to say nothing at all.

"My dear, you look positively charming," said one of the directors. She couldn't remember his name, but that probably went both ways. "I do hope you are enjoying yourself?"

"It's a very memorable party." It was, but then she remembered getting her wisdom tooth extracted and the time she'd been stuck in a lift.

"Good, good." The director's smile was as sincere as her reply. "Mark my boy, there's someone I'd like you to meet."

Elly didn't follow. Whether he was by her side or not, she wasn't sharing the evening with her husband.

Why were they doing this? It wasn't them. Not the people they used to be and not who she wanted to become. Maybe if the party hadn't been at Dover it wouldn't have bothered her, but it was and it did. What about Mark though? Her fear was that this life was what he wanted.

A small group drew her into their conversation. That was polite of them, perhaps even kind. Elly smiled as brightly as she could.

"We were talking about resolutions," she was told. The group explained how between them they hoped to raise a few rungs on the corporate ladder, planned to put more effort into ensuring the items they purchased where ethically sourced, adhere more closely to the paleo diet and ... Elly tuned out and looked around for an opportunity to swap her empty glass for a full one.

"And you?" she was asked.

"I want to be happy," Elly said. She was sure the conversation was still on plans for the future, but no one seemed to know what she meant. For a moment she considered saying she was going to visit a regression therapist or have a feng shui expert advise on interior decorating but instead she did something she hadn't done for a long time. Elly told the truth.

"I want to laugh. Laugh until I cry over nothing at all, not chuckle politely over a carefully crafted witticism. I want to look forward to real things; challenges and worries and uncertainties and hopes. Not glance sideways to be sure I'm a step ahead of the neighbours and that my car pollutes at the power plant instead of when I drive it somewhere I didn't really want to go."

She saw their looks and guessed they were thinking, 'What she wants is to cut down on the chardonnay'. Well, she wanted that too. She wanted hot chocolate with marshmallows and never mind looking up the company records first to check their social inclusion policy. And she wanted a family. Elly gasped. Not because she'd told them, she hadn't, but because she's dared to admit it to herself.

"Excuse me, I think I could do with some air," she said, probably to the relief of everyone within earshot.

Elly felt a little calmer by the time she'd negotiated her way outside. Now she'd begun with the honesty she should continue. If she worked out exactly what she wanted she could try to achieve it. Maybe that's why she and Mark were back in Dover? Fate was returning her to where they'd started their journey and giving them a second chance to travel in the right direction. Or maybe it was showing that although many would say they, with their detached house, shiny new car and promotion prospects had come a long way, in reality they hadn't even got started.

So, what she wanted was children. Had wanted them for some time, she realised. Not an unusual desire; if she'd said that a few minutes earlier her fellow partygoers would have understood. Or thought they did. Elly didn't want to produce an heir, take her statutory maternity leave and rejoin the rat-race. She wanted children to love, to play games with and watch grow. More than that she wanted a family and a home, just as she'd had when she was a child. As Mark had, three doors down on the same street. Back then bedrooms were shared with siblings, they had no idea what an ensuite was and upwardly mobile meant climbing one of the surrounding hills for a picnic.

Her resolution could be to throw away her contraceptives but, although that might result in the baby, it wouldn't produce the family. She needed help with that. Mark's help; and hadn't he always promised she'd have that?

The smokers went back inside. Elly heard one claim he'd just smoked his very last cigarette. She remembered previous New Year's resolutions of her own; lose weight, get a promotion, better golf handicap, a fitted kitchen. Mark and Elly had worked together and achieved those aims. Superficial as the results were, they showed the possibility of having what she wanted if they worked together, if it was what he wanted too. Was it?

Elly thought further back to when they were kids. Resolutions then were things like having chocolate every day for breakfast and getting a dog – which could talk and fly! Sometimes moving on and changing your priorities was the right thing.

Another guest stepped out of the hotel.

"Elly?" It was Mark and he sounded worried. "Elly are you out here?"

"Over here."

He joined her. "Are you all right?"

She didn't know. "I needed some air." Elly shivered again.

"You're cold. Do you want to come back in?"

"No. I think I'd like to go for a walk." She gestured towards the cliffs and castle.

"Let me fetch your coat and we'll go together."

He wasn't gone long, not even long enough to apologise for leaving early. Could it be that he wasn't sorry? They climbed up the cliff path, hand in hand. As they walked she did her best to explain.

"I understand," he murmured.

Did he though? And did he want the same things?

They heard the distant tinkle of ship's bells down in the harbour. "It must be midnight," Elly whispered.

"Happy New Year," Mark kissed her, then gave her one of the candy canes which had decorated the huge tree in the ballroom. "They were the closest I could get to wine gums. Will they do?"

"It depends why you've brought them. Are you looking back at the past and thinking how far we've come?" Don't let it be that.

"When we first booked the hotel for tonight that is what I thought we'd be celebrating," Mark said.

"But not now?"

"No. Now I'm looking forward to what's ahead. You spoke about us having taken a wrong turning. I don't see it like that. More a detour somewhere foreign, just to see what it was like."

"But you don't want to stay there? You're happy to go back home?"

"No, not back. Forwards. That's where our home and family are, in the future." He held up his candy cane for her to tap hers against, just as they'd done before with glasses of wine and before that with wine gums.

Elly touched hers to his, then looped it over the top so they were linked like sections in a chain. They stood looking down at the sea and out towards the future. They stood together.

23. Rebuilding Bolton Abbey

Tanya hadn't even known where she was driving until she parked her car near Bolton Abbey. The Valley of Desolation; where else could she head at a time like this? They'd visited together so many times, her and Mike. Then, when they'd been happy, the name had seemed ironic. Now it was perfectly appropriate. The dark gloomy clouds matched her mood and the wet leaves seemed to be dripping sorrowful tears. How different from the first time she'd come, more than twenty years ago.

Then she'd been young, bright and full of optimism. It had been one of those summers with just enough rain to keep the countryside fresh and green, but even that had fallen during the nights. Tanya had been on Girl Guide camp. Bored on the day trip to the abbey, she'd wandered off and bumped into Mike, or rather his tripod.

"What are you photographing?" she'd asked after apologising and being assured no harm was done.

"The abbey." He could have made the reply sarcastic, but he hadn't.

"Why? It's all ruined," she'd said.

"Of course it isn't. If it was there'd be nothing left."

Technically that was true she agreed. When she looked again, imagining the view framed in Mike's camera it no longer seemed a worthless pile of rubble, but a place with interest.

"Could it be rebuilt?" she asked.

"Sure. Can't you imagine stained glass in that window?"

She'd looked up at the broken piece of stonework and just for a moment it seemed the sun was streaming through a brightly coloured image.

"I can! And I bet there were tapestries on the walls. Religious scenes and maybe local views."

"And candles and flowers everywhere."

"Oh yes and incense in those fancy burner things. A procession and singing."

In their minds they rebuilt it, filled it with happiness. Devout but cheerful monks administering medicine and food to the poor. Weddings, Christmas feasts and special saint's days. It was all speculation but they convinced each other and knew that, in their minds at least, it would stay that way forever.

On the last day of the camp, just as they were loading the minibus, Mike arrived. He gave her a box of local biscuits and a postcard with his address on it. She wrote back to thank him, using a card from her hometown of Oxford. They became pen friends.

When other girls her age started going out with boys, Tanya stayed home to write to Mike and study history. Tanya's parents were happy then, but less pleased when she said she was going to Bradford Uni.

"You can't chose a university because it's near a boy."

"They're all near boys," Tanya pointed out. "And the facilities of this one are good."

The facilities were indeed good, as were Tanya's results. When she graduated her parents wanted to know when she was coming home.

"I am home; in Yorkshire with Mike."

Neither family were supportive when they first said they intended to marry. They were advised it would be a mistake, for them both, to marry their first crush. Everyone felt Mike would resent that Tanya earned more. Everyone was wrong. Mike was proud of her achievements. A loving husband and later a wonderful stay at home father. He was much more of a man than those of their parents' generation who were scared of what a woman might do if she were let out the kitchen.

It hadn't been Mike that had spoiled things. It'd been her. Bright, focussed Tanya. Idiot, idiot, idiot.

She'd been seduced by the southern accent she remembered when a new guy arrived at work. She'd been asked to show him round the area. Stephen was keen on photography, wanted to see local beauty spots. She could have, should have, given him a map and a few suggestions after the first day or so of orientation. Or perhaps got Mike to show him around instead. Should, but didn't.

Stephen showed her his photographs. They were beautiful and almost all were of her. Mike still took photographs, but his beautiful ones were mostly of historic buildings and dramatic scenery. The ones of her were family snaps of Tanya pregnant, or holding a baby. They showed her as a wife, a mother; not a desirable woman. Not like the way she saw herself in Stephen's pictures and reflected in his eyes. Yes, she fell for the cliché.

Tanya met Stephen after work, at weekends, whenever she could. She hadn't brought him here though, to Bolton abbey. Even for her that would have been one betrayal too many.

When he suggested they visit it, she woke up and saw

she'd risked her marriage for nothing. Nothing she couldn't have done as a teenager. They were right, the people who'd said she should have experimented more when she was younger. Then she'd have known no other man's kiss was as sweet as Mike's. No other man's touch so gentle. No other man so loved by her. Maybe then she wouldn't have lost him.

Tanya forced herself to walk into the abbey. She'd come to say goodbye, though she didn't want to leave the place, the people, Mike.

She blinked away her tears and the rain. There was a man there looking as miserable as she felt. Looking like Mike. Tears streaked his face.

She ran to him, then stopped. Why was he there?

As if he'd read the question on her face he said, "I came looking for you. I thought I knew you, that you'd come here."

He did know her. And she knew him. She'd not realised it when she set out, but she'd been hoping he'd be there.

"Can I do anything to make it right?" he asked.

"Do you want to? I've ruined everything."

"No you haven't. If it was ruined there'd be nothing left and we're still here aren't we?"

"We can rebuild our marriage?"

"We can try."

She looked up at the hole in the huge stone walls and for a minute the light caught in her falling tears and she thought she saw stained glass glowing in the window.

24. Having Your Cake

Wendy had been having that dream again. She sighed as got out of bed, what a state to be in; dreaming of chocolate éclairs. Was that what happened when you reached middle age? The exciting dreams of youth were replaced by the desire for a cream filled pastry. The worst part of it was that she knew that, just like her dreams of a glitzy career or fabulous wedding, this one wouldn't come true.

She tried to console herself that at least she'd had the pleasure of a huge corner office, floating down the aisle in a frilly confection and eating an éclair, even if they had all happened in her sleep. That didn't help; she knew her dreams just reminded her of all she was missing in real life.

Whatever she did, she just couldn't stop thinking about crisp golden choux pastry, oozing with cream. She could almost see the rich chocolate icing dripping down the sides. In her sleep, she'd pick up the éclair with one hand. Using the other, she'd reach out to wipe up a stray drop of icing and lick the sweet topping off her finger.

Of course, she had eaten and enjoyed plenty of real cream cakes in the past, that's why after months of dieting she still had more than a stone to lose.

She has a job, but years of maternity leave put paid to her hopes of promotion. She got married, in fact still is happily married, but the service had been a registry office do. There'd been no extravagant flowers, no organ music, no dress or veil. They didn't even have proper vows, just a legal service followed by a meal with their family and drinks with friends. She'd looked smart in her cream trouser suit, but she would have preferred a frothy creation of lace and silk. Paul, a Leading Hand in the Royal Navy was serving on HMS Cardiff at the time of the Gulf war. The wedding had been swiftly arranged. Wendy's relief at his safe return was ample compensation for the short service and lack of dress.

"Who wants to look like a meringue anyway?" she'd joked to friends. If they realised that an extravagant dress was exactly what she'd wanted, they kept tactfully quiet.

Meringues; why did she have to think of meringues? Everything from the cake shop was banned since she'd begun her diet. She'd managed to lose almost two stone; she wouldn't weaken now, when she was over half way towards her target weight.

Would just the one éclair really be so bad? She could go for a brisk walk to work it off and once she'd eaten it she'd stop craving cakes; wouldn't she?

At work, it was the birthday of one of the girls. She'd brought in cream cakes. There, right in front of Wendy, was a plate of cream slices, coffee doughnuts, apple turnovers and chocolate éclairs. She had to swallow several times to make sure she didn't drool.

"Whoops, sorry Wendy," the birthday girl said as she moved the cakes. "I didn't mean for you to see them. You're doing so well with your diet, I wouldn't want to tempt you."

Too late, Wendy thought, but managed a watery smile. Telling everyone about her diet had seemed a good move at first; they'd all been very supportive. She regretted it now. She decided to go out at lunchtime; it wasn't far to the bakery.

"Going out?" she was asked as she slipped on her jacket.

"Yes."

"Your salad is in the fridge, I hope you weren't thinking of sneaking of for a burger?"

"Absolutely not. No, I thought I would go for a walk, you know, burn up a few calories."

"Great idea. Mind if I come with you? I ate three cakes this morning."

Her salad didn't appeal after the walk, so Wendy just picked at her lunch. She was really hungry by the time she left work. She'd go into the supermarket and sit down in the café with a cup of tea and the longed for éclair.

She almost made it to the counter, had in fact reached out her hand for a tray, when she heard her name called. Her neighbour had spotted her. Darn it, she'd forgotten the woman worked here.

"What are you up to? For a minute it looked like you were heading for the café for something naughty, but that can't be right? Not with your diet."

"Er, no," Wendy glanced around. The CD section was closest. "I was going to look at them." She gestured at a display.

"Slobbing out in front of the sofa won't shift the pounds."

How come everyone she knew had suddenly transformed into a health and fitness expert?

"I know. I thought I'd see if you have any keep fit ones."

"You're in luck, we've got a really good range, you're bound to find something suitable."

"Oh good."

The woman insisted on chatting to Wendy until she'd

made a selection and headed to a till with it.

"What have you got there?" Paul demanded as she tried to get through the front door without her purchase being spotted.

She showed him.

"Oh, Wendy, I'm so proud of you."

After that, she had no choice but to regularly spend an hour huffing and puffing in front of the TV. Watching her perform triceps dips and inner thigh stretches seemed to encourage Paul to take his favourite kind of exercise. He pulled off her leotard and freed her hair from the ponytail.

"You're really doing well with this diet, Wendy. What with that and all the exercise, I reckon you look as good as the day I married you. I bet you could still get into your outfit too."

"Nearly, but even when I can, I don't think I'll wear it. I loved it at the time, but it would look very dated now."

"I suppose so. I tell you what, I'll buy you a really smart new outfit when you've got to your target weight. Something really special."

"Thanks, Paul."

She hugged him. It was thoughtful of him and would provide a little extra motivation, but unfortunately, it had reminded her of her disappointment at not having a wedding dress.

"Hey, what's up love? Did I say something wrong? I love you whatever size you are, you do know that?"

"Yes, of course I do."

"I'm so proud of how you've stuck to the diet. You look fabulous and I want to show everyone how delighted I am that you're my wife."

That was all very sweet, but she wasn't sure what buying her a new dress had to do with that. OK, he'd said a 'smart outfit' but Wendy was, for once, going to wear a fabulous dress. She wasn't sure when or where, but she was determined it would be as soon as possible.

For several days, she managed to push away the thoughts of a chocolate éclair. That was until she woke up with her finger in her mouth; the sleeping Wendy had been licking gooey chocolate icing from a plate of cakes. It was Saturday; she could find an excuse to slip down to the bakery.

"Would you mind if I tried your bicycle?" she asked her son.

"Tried it for what?"

"Riding of course. I, er, thought I should try different forms of exercise."

"You can if you like. The tyre might need pumping up though."

Wendy wheeled the bike onto the driveway. The front tyre was indeed a bit soft. She located the valve and turned it. There was a soft hiss as all the air escaped.

"Want a hand, Mum?"

Her son pumped up the tyre.

"How long since you rode a bike?" he asked.

"I'm not sure, but you never forget how, do you?"

"Let me get my trainers. I'll come for a jog with you, make sure you're OK."

Wendy was touched by her son's concern and support. She tried to be grateful as she peddled along next to him whilst he ran for miles and miles – and miles.

In the afternoon, Wendy drove down to the bakery. She bought a cake. She was carrying it back to the car, wondering where to go to eat it, when she was spotted by her mother-in-law.

"Wendy, what have you got there? Is that what it looks like?"

"Yes, but, er, it's not for me."

"Oh?"

"No, one of the girls at work has had a minor op. She'll be in hospital a couple of days, so I thought I'd take this to cheer her up."

"What a coincidence. I was going to the hospital to visit a friend. If it's not inconvenient, perhaps you could give me a lift?"

Not only did Wendy have to watch the boring girl from accounts devour her cake, but the visit to the hospital meant that there wasn't time for her to make the fish pie with the rich sauce and crispy potato topping that she'd planned for supper. They had to make do with grilled salmon and green salad.

Wendy had a lie-in on Sunday. She'd spent over an hour every day the last week doing some kind of exercise. It wasn't surprising that she was tired. Bleary eyed she stepped onto the scales. She got off and fetched her glasses. She got on again, then off to check that they were zeroed correctly.

"Paul!"

He came running.

"Look at that! I've only three pounds to go. I'm actually ahead of schedule."

"That's brilliant, love."

He kissed his wife, before leading her back to the

bedroom and helping her burn off a few more calories.

Wendy had the cake dream again. She knew she should ignore it; she was so close now. Somehow knowing she was ahead of schedule made her think she could relax slightly.

On the way home from work she drove through the High Street. She saw Paul's car. What was that doing here? He didn't come home this way. Her cake forgotten, she waited. Soon she saw him walking towards her. He was obviously surprised to see her. The bag he was carrying was quickly hidden behind him.

"What have you got there?"

Paul looked embarrassed. "You couldn't just forget you've seen me?"

"No, I most certainly cannot."

She grabbed at the bag. It was from a bridal shop.

"Is there something you want to tell me?"

"I didn't want to say anything whilst you were dieting. You've done so well and …"

"A bridal shop, Paul? Have you forgotten you're already married?"

"No, of course not. It's our anniversary soon. I've arranged a surprise."

"What kind of surprise?"

"You know what I said about being pleased you're my wife, wanting to show you off and buying you something new?"

"Yes."

"I've arranged for us to renew our vows. I was sure you'd hit your target weight on this Sunday's weigh in. I thought I'd tell you then and show you this."

Wendy looked in the bag.

"It's a catalogue," she said.

"For wedding dresses. I'd like to buy you a proper wedding dress. Would you mind? Our wedding was great, but I've often wished I could stand at the altar and watch you float towards me, holding a bouquet of roses, with your hair piled up and you dressed in a magnificent white lacy dress. I've imagined the organ playing the wedding march and me lifting your veil and making my vows. You'd look lovely in one of these dresses."

Wendy wiped her eyes and hugged him.

"I love you, Paul."

"And I love you." He kissed her.

"Oh, what about guests? Will people be able to come at such short notice?"

"Er, well it won't exactly be short notice for a lot of them. I sort of mentioned it to a few people. When you started dreaming about cakes, I realised you'd need some help."

Wendy tried to think who could be in on the secret. She soon realised that nearly everyone she knew had become extra supportive of her diet at around the same time.

"So when friends and family mysteriously turned up to save me from temptation, it wasn't always a coincidence?" she asked.

Paul grinned at her. "Anyway, what are you doing here; this isn't on your way home."

Wendy knew she'd stopped in town to buy something, but couldn't remember what.

25. Waiting For An Answer

"No, no, no," I wailed as I saw my grades for the essay I'd done on the Mayor of Casterbridge.

Apart from a short time, when I thought there weren't enough, there have always been too many Thomas Hardys in my life. I failed English Lit because of one of them.

"Are you ever going to give me an answer, Sharon?" was a favourite question of teachers, as I spent lessons dreaming and fantasising over Thomas.

Not the author of course, but the rugby player of the same name in the upper sixth form. He was totally gorgeous. Just about as gorgeous as I considered myself in fact. I might as well admit right now that I'm still sometimes a bit 'me me me' and was much worse back then. Although I wasn't very nice I still managed, at times, to have a far too high opinion of myself. All the girls fancied Thomas which, looking back, might be why I wanted him myself.

One of our school trips was to Corfe Castle, down in Dorset. I wasn't studying history, but my best mate Melanie was. Spending the day with her sounded more fun than lessons, so I talked my way into one of the spare seats on the coach. Probably the teachers were pleased I seemed to be showing an interest in anything vaguely educational.

On the way, we stopped for a quick look at Hardy's monument. I knew the area was sometimes referred to as 'Hardy Country' because the author set many of his stories there and assumed the monument was to him.

"I'm sure you're not the only person who's made that mistake, Sharon," said Dan.

He was a student teacher on placement with our school. Melanie liked him, said he was fun and really good at explaining things. To me he was just another teacher, therefore booor-ring. I'd given him the nickname 'desperate Dan' after his attempts to get me engaged in lessons.

Dan continued, "In fact this tower was erected in honour of Thomas Masterman Hardy, hero of the battle of Trafalgar ..."

I'd spotted an information sign by then and worked it out, so interrupted with, "And Nelson's right hand man."

"Oh, very good, Sharon!"

Dan did look as though he thought I'd said something clever, or at least funny, but I wasn't really sure if he was praising or ridiculing me. Either way, the whole thing had made me feel uncomfortable. I set to work making Dan squirm.

That was easy. The poor sap had already used the word 'erected' and went on to refer to the tower's size and the hardness of the rock. It doesn't take much to get teenage girls giggling. Dan was redder than my cherry lipgloss long before I'd got to 'kiss me Hardy!'

A few weeks later, the young and gorgeous Thomas Hardy invited me to the end of year disco. There were no proms back then; a tape deck in the sports hall was as glam as it got. I wasn't going to go. At sixteen I was way too cool; but arriving with Thomas Hardy would make a difference. I bullied and cajoled all my mates into going to witness my triumph. No point finally getting the guy if nobody knew about it, was there?

My hoped for moment of glory turned to humiliation when Thomas failed to arrive. I was furious! There I was all pulled in, pushed up and totally let down.

I decided to stay home and if anyone asked, say Thomas had taken me somewhere better.

"Don't answer it," I yelled at dad when the phone rang. Then as he went out into the hall anyway, I said, "If it's for me say I'm out."

"Hello, Melanie," he said. "Yes, she is. Hold on a tick. Sharon, it's for you!"

As if that wasn't bad enough he stood right next to me when I answered and loudly said he would give me a lift in if I still wanted to go. Of course after that there was no getting out of it.

It was awful; everyone knew I'd been stood up. Dan asked me to dance. I thought that was OK, it's not like he was a proper teacher and he wasn't bad looking in a boring kind of way. But then he went and danced with all the other girls who couldn't get a date.

"Gee thanks. Show me up as one of the losers why don't you?" I said when he came to ask again.

"He was just trying to be nice," Melanie said when she came round a few days later.

"But he did the same to everyone! Why would he do that?"

"Because he's a nice person?"

"You're always sticking up for people," I said. "Perhaps you can explain why Thomas Hardy made me look a complete idiot?"

"Perhaps he got the wrong day?"

"For a school disco at his own school? I don't think so."

"Maybe he's ill?"

"I hope it's something painful."

"He got knocked over, fell into a coma and is lying there awake but unable to communicate hoping you'll come to his bedside?" She threw herself onto the sofa to demonstrate.

"It'd be in the papers or on the news," I said and never mind I never watched or read anything so dull. Still she had cheered me up and when she suggested we go into town and see if we could find any shops looking for staff, I grabbed my bag and headed out.

I got taken on as a waitress. Dan was one of my first customers and I messed up his order. My boss must have seen his surprise when I placed a full English in front of him rather than the teacake and coffee he'd ordered, because she came over to ask if there was anything wrong.

"Not at all," Dan said. "This looks delicious."

I was nearly sure he winked at me. When he came back in the next day, I asked him what he'd like.

"Why don't you surprise me?" he said.

It became a bit of a joke between us, with me selecting the strangest food combinations I could think of and him over acting either horrified shock or amazed delight, depending on whether or not my boss was within sight of him.

By the time she said to me, "You could take you break when your friend comes in if you like and sit and have a cup of tea with him," I had no desire to snap that he wasn't my friend.

It didn't take many conversations with Dan to discover Melanie was right and he was actually a very nice person. One I found both interesting and fun. Suppose I'd grown up a little bit by then. We became good friends and then something more than that.

Melanie and I stayed friends. Her interest in history eventually led to her getting a job on HMS Victory, the ship Thomas Hardy had captained at Trafalgar.

"Who'd have guessed I'd be the one spending my days with Thomas Hardy and you'd end up as teacher's pet?" she joked.

"It is odd. Wonder if I'm ill or something? I've been feeling peculiar these last few days."

When I told Dan I was pregnant, he immediately asked me to marry him.

"What? No, no I don't want to get married."

"Think about it at least."

I saw how hurt he was and felt terrible about that as I did care as a friend and didn't want my friend hurt. Everyone, especially my parents and Melanie, said I was mad to say no. They thought marrying the father of my child, a good man with a good job who cared about me and whom I cared about was the perfect solution. I could see the logic of that, but still I turned him down again and again. I was sure that if I agreed I'd feel trapped and only let him down later, decide an intimate friend wasn't enough, or fall in love for real and then when we split up he'd be really devastated. Besides, what did someone clever like him see in me? Who's to say he wouldn't soon loose interest, just like Thomas Hardy had?

It wasn't easy being a single mother but I really thought I was doing the right thing and not just for myself. Dan gave me money for Saffron and spent lots of time with her. He was the best father he could be at the distance I kept him. Of course our easy friendship suffered, but we remained on good terms. He gave her away when she married and after we'd danced together, Dan once again asked me to marry him.

"When are you going to stop asking me that?" was all the answer he got.

"When you say yes."

He asked about once a year, so I suppose it had happened four more times when my neighbour said she was moving.

"I'll miss you," I said and meant it. We'd always got on quite well, letting in workmen, watering the garden and borrowing pints of milk.

"Not once you see Thomas Hardy you won't!"

"Who?"

"That's the name of the chap who's bought this place. Single, tall, dark hair, rather good looking, about your age. I'm doing you a favour moving really!"

I rang Melanie in a panic; she was the one person who'd known how much I'd liked Thomas and how much I'd been hurt when he stood me up.

"It was a long time ago, Sharon," she reminded me. "You're both more than twice the age you were then. If he's changed in the same way you have, he'll feel bad about how he treated you."

I thought she was right. A while ago I overheard a girl turn down a boy in an unnecessarily harsh manner and I'd cringed at the memory of doing the same kind of thing myself.

"So what do I do?"

"Are you still, you know, interested in him?"

"No, I was cured of that the night of the disco."

"OK then. I'd just pretend it never happened. There's no good living in the past."

"You're the last person who should be saying that! You do it all day every day on that old ship of yours."

"It's not the same. Tell me, what do you think about Thomas Hardy the writer?"

"Dull," I said though I couldn't see how it was relevant.

"Even though you're judging him on the one book we read at school and you've never even looked at another?"

"You sound like, Dan."

"Wouldn't hurt you to listen to him now and then. Anyhow, what about the other famous man of the same name?"

"Desperate Dan? … oh, you mean Captain Hardy?"

"There you go. He was a Captain at one time, but before that he was a lieutenant and after rose to admiral. You think of him in the way you first learned about him. It's the same with this guy. How nice a person were you as a teenager?"

I knew the answer to that one. "I was immature, self-centred and selfish."

"And boys develop more slowly than girls so are you really being fair to judge him on that time? Besides there might well have been a reason he had to stand you up."

"Yep, he's been in a coma for twenty years, just come out of it and bought a house next door to the girl he was going to take to the school disco the night he was hit on the head."

"Possibly. Or toothache perhaps?"

"That's not fair!"

She'd named an excuse I myself had used once to get out

of going to something with Dan and Saffron.

"That was a very long time ago now. I've begun to realise how lucky I am to still have him, not just in my daughter's life, but in my own."

"You have?"

"Of course. Dan is one of the good guys and I'll give Thomas Hardy a chance to prove he is too."

"But just as a neighbour, yes? I don't want you to go getting hurt again."

I looked out for him from behind my bedroom curtains when the furniture lorry arrived. The description I'd been given was accurate; the man was attractive and still had thick dark hair, but he'd changed a lot. I wasn't at all sure I'd have known him if I hadn't been told who he was. It wasn't long before he came round and introduced himself. When I gave my own name there wasn't the slightest flicker of recognition.

"He didn't even remember me, Mel. How rude is that?" I said on the phone that night.

"I'm surprised," she admitted. "You haven't changed very much. He either treated a lot of girls badly or he's got a terrible memory. Maybe both."

"Are you OK, Mel?"

"Fine, why?"

"You always look for the best in everyone. I expected you to say he must have bad eyes, or felt so ashamed he couldn't bring himself to admit what he'd done."

"I suppose it could be something like that, but there's also the possibility he really isn't very nice."

"Who are you and what have you done with Melanie?"

"I'm your best friend who doesn't want you hurt. Talking of which, have you seen Dan lately?"

"You going to tell me he's horrible and to keep away from him?"

"No. Dan's a sweetie. Far too good for the likes of you."

"True."

"I didn't really mean that."

I knew she didn't, which meant her warning about Thomas Hardy got me thinking. Not for long though as Saffron brought round her daughter the next day and left her with me whilst she ran a few errands.

Seems impossible, I'm not yet quite forty, still feel like a girl and already I'm a grandmother. Something else hard to believe is how much I love that little girl. She means just as much to me as her mother does.

We played out in the garden, a mad game involving the wearing of silly hats and running round her teddies in circles. When a double glazing salesman called, although I soon sent him packing, I was glad of a chance to catch my breath.

"Nanna's going to get some juice, would you like some?"

"Yes please, Nanna."

I thought she'd followed me into the kitchen, but when I looked up from filling the glasses I saw her toddling down the path – and that the salesman had left the gate open. Ours isn't a busy road, but because of that cars sometimes drive down it far too fast. I dropped the glasses and ran.

I wasn't quick enough to stop her reaching the road, but Thomas Hardy was. By the time I reached them he was holding her high in the air. Of course I should have been grateful he'd stopped her before she was in danger from the traffic, but I wasn't thinking straight and the poor kid was screaming her head off.

"How dare you scare my darling girl!" I yelled at him. I'd raised my hand to slap him when I realised she was shrieking with laughter not fear. His intention had been to help, not harm her. I felt stupid, not quite as stupid as I did when I was stood up at the school disco, but this time the fault was entirely mine.

"I'm really sorry, I saw her heading for the road and panicked. Adrenaline kicked in I suppose and …"

"That's all right, no harm done." He lowered her to the ground, just inside my fence and she trotted back towards her toys.

"How about we call it quits?" I suggested.

He gave a puzzled frown.

"Don't you remember me from school?" I asked.

"Er no, but I went to an all boys. If you went there you've changed a lot."

"Another Thomas Hardy! I've always said there are too many of them … " Naturally I felt even more of an idiot then. I apologised again and explained a little.

When he called his namesake an idiot for standing me up, I warmed to him. I'm pretty sure he'll be a good neighbour and perhaps a friend. He'll also be a subtle memory that I haven't always been the nicest person. Anything to do with any of the Thomas Hardys has the power to make me feel bad about myself in some way.

There are plenty of people who make me feel good about myself. There's Melanie who always looks for, and finds, the best in people. More importantly there's my beloved Saffron and darling granddaughter. And there's Dan. Almost everything good in my life has come from him. I didn't know where that thought came from, but it hit me hard that I loved him. The way I'd treated him I probably didn't deserve to be loved in return but I was.

"Excuse me," I said to Thomas. "I have a call to make."

I rang Dan from the garden so I could keep watch over our granddaughter. "You know that question you keep on asking? Well, don't ask me again."

"Sharon, I said there was only one way you could make me stop."

"Yes, I remember. Yes, yes, yes."

Thank you for reading this book. I hope you enjoyed it. If you did, I'd really appreciate it if you could leave a short review on Amazon and/or Goodreads.

To learn more about my writing life, hear about new releases and get a free exclusive ebook, sign up to my newsletter – subscribepage.io/ItLSNa or you can find the link on my website patsycollins.co.uk

More books by Patsy Collins

Little Mallow cosy mystery series

Disguised Murder and Community Spirit in Little Mallow
Dependable Friends and Deceitful Neighbours
in Little Mallow
Deadly Words and Innocent Gossip in Little Mallow

Other novels

Firestarter
Escape To The Country
A Year And A Day
Paint Me A Picture
Leave Nothing But Footprints
Acting Like A Killer

Non-fiction

From Story Idea To Reader
(co-written with Rosemary J. Kind)

A Year Of Ideas:
365 sets of writing prompts and exercises

Short story collections

Over The Garden Fence
Up The Garden Path
Through The Garden Gate
In The Garden Air
Beyond The Garden Gate

No Family Secrets
Can't Choose Your Family
Keep It In The Family
Family Feeling
Happy Families

All That Love Stuff
Lots Of Love
Love Is The Answer

Slightly Spooky Stories I
Slightly Spooky Stories II
Slightly Spooky Stories III

Slightly Spooky Stories IV
Slightly Spooky Stories V

Just A Job
Perfect Timing
A Way With Words
Dressed To Impress
Coffee & Cake
Not A Drop To Drink
Criminal Intent
Crime In Mind
Days To Remember
Making A Move
A Clean Bill Of Health
Your Good Health